LITTLE GLORY

LITTLE GLORY

ROGER PINCKNEY

Wyrick & Company
Charleston

For Susan.
If these words were diamonds, I'd lay them at your feet.

Published by Wyrick & Company
Post Office Box 89
Charleston, SC 29402

Printed in the United States of America

Library of Congress Cataloging-in-Publication Data

First Edition

Chapter One

Jesus said "Seek ye the Truth and the Truth will set you free." When Pilate asked "What is Truth?" Jesus didn't answer. So I won't either. But I can tell you this much: For pure cussed outrageousness, the truth beats a lie every time. And I can tell you about what I heard and what I saw when I was growing up in Calhoun County, South Carolina, a long, long time ago, when there was smoke on the water and spirits on the wind.

You can believe it if you want to. It's true enough for me.

You can call me Little Mac. I ain't little any more, and I ain't young either, but when your daddy was Sheriff Mac McCloud, you'll be Little Mac forever, even if you grow seven feet, top three hundred pounds, and outlive Methuselah.

My given name is Malcolm Edward McCloud VII. I don't brag about the seventh part too much. Daddy was the sixth. Granddaddy the fifth, and so on, back to a granddaddy with more greats than I know what to do with—a Scot sergeant in the British Army, a drinking, whoring rascal, they say. He came to Charleston in 1777 to fight Indians and when he found out we was English just like him, he swapped sides. After the war, he traveled from Georgia to Virginia with a thoroughbred stallion and bred up the local mares with racing foals. He bred up the local girls, too, and died in a tomahawk fight up in the Cherokee country.

Somewhere along the line, he stopped long enough to give a man-child his last name and it has careened down the generations to me.

I got the name from the McClouds and some of the grit, I guess, but not much else. We got the plantation from my daddy's mother, who married a Heyward from the family that signed the Declaration. They were quality, and as near as I can tell, none of us McClouds were much worth a damn until they got Heyward blood in them. But, then, the Heywards had been marrying their cousins so long, they were about run down to nothing, and McCloud blood did them good, too.

The Heywards owned five rice plantations up on the blackwater Little Glory River: ten thousand acres and a thousand slaves. When old Thomas G. Heyward signed right under where it said "all men are created equal," I like to think he told his buddy Tom Jefferson about what it meant down on Little Glory Plantation.

The Heywards hired a Quaker schoolmarm two months a year, a preacher one Sunday a month, and gave the slaves free run of larder and livestock each Christmas. The Heywards figured out the task system, how long it would take a good man to get each job done. The young and the old and the women were rated, three-quarters task and half task, and so on. When a slave got his task done, he could knock off and work on his own.

The Heywards ate pretty good from vegetables and chickens and pigs bought from their own slaves. Heyward slaves took the money and wandered over and bought things from the neighbor slaves and that got everybody stirred up and pretty soon the whole country roundabouts took up the task system and the planters along the Little Glory, the Big Glory, and the Tullifinny Rivers became the richest men in South Carolina.

Four score and seven years later, when General Sherman's bummers rode through the country shouting "All you niggers is free," most of them smiled and said "That's right" and kept on hoeing their gardens and tending their hogs and fishing down on the rice canals. I know this won't stick with some folks these days, but it's the God's truth.

I heard a story once and if it ain't true, it sure ought to be. Sometime in the 1850s Sherman pulled duty in Charleston and got tangled up with some planter's daughter, a Ravenel girl, I believe she was. He was just a red-headed Yankee lieutenant and she spoke French and was high toned and snippish, but when the ladies of Charleston entertained the officers from Fort Moultrie, everybody got into their juleps and he had her in the oleanders behind a house on Tradd Street.

He was mighty impressed and asked for her hand. She said yes but her daddy said Sherman was just one more damn Yankee who would never 'mount to much and the girl went with daddy and the money and the land and Sherman swore someday he'd bring the women of the South to the washboard.

You seen the pictures, all lean-faced and skinny and mad, like you get from nibbling No-Doze and sipping Air Wick. But they didn't have either back in those days, so it might have been that Ravenel girl that ruint him. If her daddy could have seen what was coming, he would have said "Hell, yes, take this girl" and maybe thrown in a plantation or two in the bargain. But he didn't and we all got burnt out.

They say you could see Sherman coming for miles. Sixty thousand men in four columns, each covering a swath forty miles wide. From Atlanta to Savannah to Columbia they came, a plague of blue locusts upon the land, eating all they could, destroying the rest.

The Good Book tells you about no rich or poor, no male or female, no slave no free. You'll wait a long time seeing it here on earth, but they saw it on the Little Glory River in January of 1865. All God's chillen at the edge of the creek, black and white and young and old and men and women, watching the plumes upon the horizon—the Fripp place, the Stoneys', Lesesnes' and Framptons' places, each new smoke closer than the last.

The Yankees burnt Little Glory, too, burnt the rice mill and the barns and the big house on the high bluff above the river. My great-grandmother wouldn't leave the house and went after one Yankee with a curtain rod. Then they threw kerosene on her and said "Lady, get out or we'll fire you, too."

So she did.

But when the young captain with the torching squad got down to the tabby cabins along the slave street, a curious thing happened. I don't expect you'll believe me, but go look in the February 2, 1865, edition of *Frank Leslie's Illustrated Weekly* and see for yourself. There you'll find a sketch of the Little Glory big house going up in flames, and then a bend in the river and a line of shanties off in the live oaks and a bunch of Yankees held up before what looks like a Mardi Gras parade. The text reads: "On the trail with General Sherman. Captain Reynolds of the Fifty-fifth Massachusetts was met by a crowd of contrabands as he approached the Negro quarter, which implored him with intense gesticulation to spare their humble dwellings. After much incantation and drumming, as these wretches are wont, Captain Reynolds heeded their request, but required their attendance at services delivered by the regimental chaplain."

Daddy told it another way. The Fifty-fifth Massachusetts was a colored outfit—white officers, and free Negroes from Boston. The Yankee generals had used them pretty hard, throwing them into fire too deadly for white men, at Charleston and Port Royal and Honey Hill, where they got bogged down in a marshy cove and the rebels stacked them like cordwood. By the end of the war, the Boston Negroes were about shot out and their replacements were former slaves who thought they'd get forty acres and a mule for fighting for the Yankees.

The procession out to meet them was led by my great-grandfather's man, John Domingo. John Domingo was pure blood—a blue gum, we say down here—a genuine *Wanderer* Negro, come over on the last boat of wild Africans in 1858. First, they put him in the rice field, but a man's hat blew off and John Domingo picked it up and gave it back. Two days later, the man turned up a nest of moccasins and got bit and died. Then, John took a drink from the pump and the next man to drink got sucked into a culvert and drowned. Pretty soon, word got out John Domingo had the Death Touch and nobody would work with him anymore. My great-grandfather had to give him his own shack on the edge of the tupelo swamp where he took up conjuring full time.

John Domingo kept his hair up in little knots to keep away the witches, wore ten pounds of rings and bracelets and anklets of Congo silver, and carried a snake-head walking stick. That Yankee captain would have had to pull his pistol on his own men to make them take another step.

After the Yankees thinned out, and great-grandpa got back from the Confederate Army, he raked the big house bricks out of the ashes and built another one, smaller, a little closer to the water. That's the house I was born in and where I sit right now writing all this down, looking out at the Little Glory River.

But I'm getting ahead of myself.

What happened after the war was worse than the fighting, worse than the losing. Some years before, Congressman Preston Brooks, a distant uncle on my mother's side, got into some trifling argument with Senator Charles Sumner of Massachusetts. Brooks got his blood up and beat Sumner nearly to death with his cane right there in the Senate hallway. After the war, Sumner, all crippled up and mean, made it pretty hot for folks down here. There was swindling and stealing and stuffing ballot boxes and my other uncle Henry McCloud shot two Yankee officers and had to run off to Brazil. I got cousins down there, I guess, and I figured maybe someday I'd go look them up. But now I'm too damn old for that kind of travelling.

So, the Yankees took the land for back taxes and turned it

over to the Negroes, but soon enough Congress took most of it back and gave it to the carpetbaggers. If you wanted your land back from them, you had to come up with four or five years taxes, or prove you did not serve in the Confederate Army. Great-grandpa couldn't do either. When it was all over, his ten thousand acres had shrunk to one hundred, several large piles of ashes, ruined fields, upwards of ten thousand burnt brick, and about two hundred people who somehow thought he would still be able to take care of them.

Everybody but old John Domingo. He kept up his lonesome ways, picking mushrooms and herbs and praying on the full moon like his mother had taught him. In time, he gathered quite a clientele. Snakebit or axe cut, love sick, took sick, or trouble with the law, John Domingo was your man. He told a woman she was made of rubber and she started jumping til it took three men to hold her down. He called a man a jackass and the man brayed for a week. He gave another man the slobbering fits and the man drooled and shook his head and threw his spit all over the wall til he dehydrated and died.

When great-grandpa got a sawmill going and was finally starting to make a little money again and the union men came down from New York and got the help to strike for better pay, great-grandpa hired John Domingo and pretty soon the sawyers, skidders, and timber cruisers were glad to work again for ten cents less per day.

Later on, when the crop failed and the planters had to pay in scrip and the riots broke out, John Domingo swapped sides and beat the drum for the Negroes and they stampeded the field bosses up into a little stockade by Sugar Hill Landing. The bosses held back the mob at rifle point for a day and a half until the militia finally got off the train at Yemassee and rescued them. Old John Domingo had them so worked up, Daddy said, the women would throw themselves on the ground and snap at it like runover dogs, but they dared not rush the rifles. They danced and chanted:

> *T. G. Heyward, don't know,*
> *What we told you at the sto'.*
> *All we want is greenbacks.*

They got a crop the next year and the schooners came up the Little Glory once again and threw their ballast stones upon the banks and took on cask after cask of rice and everybody got paid cash for a few years. But then the storm of '93 came through with a twenty-foot surge and drowned two thousand and breached the dikes and let in the sea, poisoning the fields for a generation.

So my great-grandfather died, and ten years later my grandfather died and they buried them both in the Stoney Creek Cemetery along the north dike of the Little Glory fields where the mournful oaks throw their branches out over the water and the Spanish moss hangs like long gray strings of tears. The river was high both of those years, Daddy said, and the coffins floated in the graves, then blubbered and sank when two men who had survived war and riot and ruin finally went down.

But when John Domingo died, they planted him out in the woods and nobody will say quite where. They buried most of him, anyway. His fingers and toes and his rings and little knots of his hair got passed from here to Savannah among a great throng of disciples. They're probably still out there somewhere, dusty little knots of hair and yellow and gristly bits of bones rattling around in root doctor conjure bags, working magic we know is true, even though we can't explain it.

And his snake-head cane? Well, I know right where that is, but I'll get to that after awhile.

I don't want you to think I'm bragging. This was all before my time and I did not have a thing to do with it. But all this blood and war and voodoo laps over onto me, and it laps over onto my boy, Malcolm Edward McCloud VIII. It's in our bones by now and we couldn't shake it even if we wanted. But we take no credit for it. We took what we got in God's private crapshoot, that's all.

But let me tell you, we got a lot.

We got Little Glory Plantation. We got blue water. We got black water. We got sunny green islands and beaches shining like polished brass. We got the seawind whispering secrets in the palmettos and the mullet flashing silver in the shallows and the ospreys falling among them like feathered lightning. We got the great rafts of sea ducks, bobbing black and white out beyond the surf line, and the moon slipping up over the edge of the world like a pirate doubloon. We got the crashing surf and the big fish and the quail whistling out in the blackberry thickets and sneaky old bucks and tom turkeys and those damn wild hogs.

And I got Sheriff Mac McCloud for a daddy and Miss Marzette after I lost my momma and I got old Doctor Indigo, who saved me when I was hog-cut and fixing to die.

And I got the story and it's a damn good one and I still got the breath to tell it.

So I will tell you.

Chapter Two

"Lil Mac! Lil Mac!" It was Miss Althea calling. Miss Althea—you say it Al-THEE-a—took care of me after momma died trying to have me a little brother. And it's *Miz*, even though you spell it Miss. So I never had any trouble calling cantankerous women "Ms.," 'cause I been doing it all my life.

I can close my eyes and still see her—not my momma, all I can remember is a soft touch and a smell like ripe peaches—but Miss Althea, barrel-round and Congo black, hands on her hips, bellering like I was a calf that needed to come home.

"Lil Mac! Lil Mac!"

Miss Althea was Little Glory born and raised. Her momma cooked for my grand-momma and I guess if you wanted to sit and figure, you probably could say her family was on Little Glory from the beginning.

I was down along the creek, fifty yards from the house, trying to rustle up a pail of shrimp and some fiddler crabs. It was early summer, 1942. There was a war going and you couldn't get gas and you couldn't get sugar and you couldn't get tires. But I didn't give a damn. I was nine years old and the puppy drum were running and Daddy was going to take me fishing.

"Lil Mac! Lil Mac! Whoo-whoo Lil Mac!"

It was one of those days like the ones that come to you in dreams. The tide was out and the mud was popping and the cotton ball clouds were way up overhead and the pungo mud was all over my feet. I was inheritor of all this, half angel, half animal, all man-child, shrimp and little fish surging before me as I stalked the shallows.

"Lil Mac! Answer me, chile! Them gator gone get you!"

It was a joke when I was nine, but it wasn't when I was six, when Miss Althea kept me close to the house by coming at me wild-eyed and fierce, working her arms like a giant pair of jaws, snap, snap, and I would holler and run inside and slide beneath the table where she was too fat to follow. And I would keep away from the riverbank for a week, or so.

"Yo daddy looking for you!"

I was three steps inside the front door and she met me in the hall, wid 'struction face, which has more in common with *de*struction than *con*struction. "Boy, what's wrong with you? Look what you done!"

I turned and looked at the footprints. Left print pungo black, right print blood red. I had nicked myself scrambling up the creek bank.

I sat on the back steps, my feet in a washtub of soapy water, soon the color of the Little Glory River when the sun slides down behind the cypress and tupelo. Miss Althea knelt at my feet, mumbling how I had no sense at all, walking out there without my bogging shoes and how she had enough cooking and washing and cleaning for one grown man and one half-grown boy and she didn't have time for no doctoring. But when she dosed the cut with turpentine, and dressed it with a long strip she had torn away from a used-up bedsheet, I would feel the love in her hands.

Althea took a final wrap, tied off the excess in a neat little square knot, then slapped me on the thigh hard enough to hurt. "Go long with you, now. You come back to this house in one piece, you hear?"

I grabbed the bait bucket and hobbled out to the shed to catch up with Daddy. There he was, getting ready for the river.

I suppose he wasn't much to look at, being sheriff and all. He was strong but short, with a scrubbly little mustache and a shock of average color hair. He'd spent a lot of time on the river and you could see it in the lines of his face.

Daddy didn't smile much, but beneath a bushy set of eyebrows, his eyes were shining blue and lightning quick. When he was heading my way and I needed to know if he was about to give me a new dog or a new fishing pole or a good switchin', his eyes would tell me all I needed to know.

The skiff was in the back of the pickup and he was fiddling with the tackle, rigging floats and hooks to dangle where the puppy drum streak in over the shell rakes on the rising water. "Lo, bub," he said, very briefly looking up. "You got us bait?"

I held up the bucket. "A dozen shrimp and twenty fiddlers."

His eyes told me I was short. Then they softened some. "What happened to that foot?"

"Oyster shell," I said.

He considered that for a second or two. "They sharp as razors, you know. Miss Althea patch you up?"

"Yessir, and she gave me a good cussing."

Daddy nodded. "Little boys need a good cussing sometimes."

"Yessir," I said, "but she don't have to be so painful about it."

Then it was Miss Althea again, bellering for the sheriff. "Just a second," Daddy said. "You reckon you can finish rigging?"

Daddy was a long time getting back. I rigged the lines like he had showed me, a button off an old shirt to stop the cork, a half ounce sinker to keep the bait down, a twenty inch leader with a sharp new hook. I untangled the anchor line and made sure both oarlocks were in the boat. I drew a jug of water from the well and stashed it under the stern seat. I found a flashlight in case we come home in the dark and beat on it til it worked. Then there was nothing else to do but wait, so I climbed into the cab and started fiddling with the radio.

There was something about some fighting in Africa, a squalling like a Hawaiian guitar gone crazy, a great blast of static, then a commercial for Wild Rose hair pomade, and finally news of Reverend Billy Kinkaid's Miracle Holy Ghost Soul Saving Revival, scheduled for the following Saturday at 7:00 P.M., right across the road from the Hercules dynamite factory, just a little south of Brunswick, Georgia. There would be singing and healing and speaking in tongues and the elders from the First United Church of Jesus Christ for all People would be picking up serpents.

I got all creepy thinking about them Pentecostals wrapping up in rattlers and copperheads and putting the snake heads in their mouths and slobbering over them like they do, so I must have jumped three feet when Daddy stuck his head in the pick-up window. "Better turn them shrimp and fiddlers aloose," he said. "I got to go."

I got to go. That's what he always said. Momma had to go too, but I was too young to remember her saying it. Daddy was going off to do his duty. In time I would love him for it, but not now.

"You said we were going fishing," I said.

"I know, son, but I got to go." I could tell he didn't like it much better than I did. "There's trouble on Williman Island."

So instead of fishing with Daddy, I raced fiddlers with Harley Davidson. Harley was Miss Althea's boy, a year older than me. There weren't any white kids on Little Glory, no colored kids either, so when school let out, all we had was each other. Even after school took in each fall and he went to his and I went to mine, sometimes he would sneak out early and wait for me in the bushes so we could go fishing or crabbing, or just bogging out in the marsh.

"Don't you go hoggin' them blue backs," Harley said. We were down on the creek bank, where a little sandbar juts out when the river takes off to the southwest, right about where Captain Reynolds and his Yankee bummers got held up by old John Domingo. Blue backs had this little Chinese looking design on their shells. They could grab ahold of you with their one big claw. It didn't hurt too bad, but if it surprised you, you'd turn them loose. They would run circles around black fiddlers, and I had just beat Harley out of a dime.

I had scribed a three-foot circle with my big toe. And we each chose a fiddler, set them in the middle and turned them loose at the same time. First fiddler out of the circle was worth ten cents. The losing fiddler got chucked in the creek, the winner got to run again, if we could catch him. Next time, Harley Davidson got his blue back and retrieved his dime.

"Where your daddy gone?" he asked. He was rummaging through the bottom of the pail, trying to corral the last of the blue backs.

"Williman Island," I said.

Harley whistled and shook his head. "You know 'bout that place?"

"Sure. You can't get there from here. You got to go to Savannah and catch the steamer. There's wild ponies there and wild n...."

I was about to say niggers, just out of habit. Daddy said only poor white trash talked that way and he would thrash me for using it and so would Miss Althea. I guess I picked it up in school. A nigger could call another nigger a nigger til it thunders and nobody would give a damn. But a white man? If you were older, you'd better be ready to fight. If you were younger, you'd get a thrashing.

"Yessir, Mr. Lil Mac, there's wild niggers there, too." He cornered a fiddler and laid it in the center of the circle, pinned it to the sand, but the fiddler took hold of his thumb and

Harley turned him loose before I was ready with my brown one.

We were running low on fiddlers. "Damnit, Harley," I said. I'd get a thrashing for cussing, too. Daddy cussed, but said I mustn't take it up til I was old enough to do it justice.

"I'm sorry Mr. Lil Mac, that thing pinched the living shit out of me."

Harley was experimenting with cussing, too. We grinned like a couple of possums. "What you reckon your Daddy doing on Williman Island?"

"Damn hell if I know."

Harley cut me another grin. "Bet he's after that damn boot-legger."

"What damn bootlegger?"

All of a sudden Harley got dead serious. "You know, what's his name?"

Colored folks around here have a couple hundred years practice dodging questions from pesky white people. *Buckra*, they call us in private, which is about the same as the word I'd get thrashed for using. Daddy said it's African, from some sort of pasty little cake they made on the other side, which is right on the money, seeing how so many white people look like bis-cuits.

"Hell no, I don't know what's his damn name."

"I forget um myself," Harley said and that was the end of it.

So we raced the last of the fiddlers and the sun slid down the west, all big and bloody over the tupelo and soft maple, the edge of my little world in 1942. And the light brimmed and spilled out over the Little Glory rice fields, spreading and deepening from pink to purple to beyond human sight. And then the hoot owls started talking about us way out in the swamp and Harley Davidson and I decided it was time to go home.

I ate by myself in the dining room, Harley and Miss Althea in the kichen, grits, the summer's first tomatoes, and fried mullet she got from her outside man, Willie Simmons. Miss Althea was First African Baptist and didn't cotton to divorce. Even though Harley's pa got Philly Fever and had run north a couple of years before, Willie Simmons would always be her outside man. He brought her mullet and venison and field corn and she made him sausage and cornbread, and cooked his grits, if you know what I mean.

So they ate and I ate and none of us spoke while the June bugs ricocheted off the window screens and the moon came up over the pines and the seawind freshened and the palmettoes rattled like Ezekiel's dry bones.

Later, when I lay in bed and the moon lit up the yard til you could see the moving shadows of the Spanish moss, and the gators started up like giant toothy bullfrogs and the chuckwills-widow called and called its name way out in the woods, above it all I could hear Miss Althea singing her way to the old slave street saved by John Domingo so long ago, singing the old songs to keep back the spirits:

> *When I went down to the river to pray,*
> *Studying about that good old way,*
> *And who shall wear that starry crown.*
> *Oh, Lord, show me the way.*

Chapter Three

It was two in the morning when Daddy finally got home. I heard the pickup rattle across the cow guard at the end of the road, the gears whining through the sand wallows, the rattle over the oak roots at the edge of the yard, and, finally, the little click when he eased the door shut so he wouldn't wake me. Then there was the creaking of the stairs and the little sliver of light beneath my door when he turned on the light in the hall.

"Daddy?" I said.

He stuck his head in the door. "You still awake, bub?"

"Yessir. You a long time getting home."

He sighed. "Yeah. I'm plumb wore out." He turned, but I called him back.

"Daddy?"

"What you want, boy?"

"Tell me a story."

"A story? You got ten cents?"

I sat up and fetched Harley Davidson's dime from beneath my pillow. It caught the light and shined like a tiny moon.

"Yessir."

"Damn if you don't, boy, damn if you don't." He limped to the bed and I squiggled over and he sat down. He smelled like sweat and tobacco and smoke from the wood-fired steamboat.

Daddy told stories better than anybody. I could write til I laid down and died and not tell you half of them. About the meteor that come ripping out of the east and lit the night like day and exploded way out in the Savannah River swamp. About the devilfish under the Port Royal dock and the great earth-quake of '86 and all the storms and wars and big tides in between.

When I was young, I figured all this was Gospel Truth. When I got a little older, I said well wait a minute now, Daddy might have taken license with some of the details. But I read and I read and I listened to a whole bunch of people I trusted one hell of a lot less than I trusted him. Now, I'm right back where I started.

So I guess I can just buck up and tell you what he said next.

Daddy paused a second, "Well, son, today I seen a man walk on the water."

OK, Daddy had religion. He didn't get plunged in the creek when he was thirteen, didn't go down in the water and see turtles and think they was Jesus and he didn't go into tongues like some folks do. But he loved God and loved his neighbors and if you've read the book, you'll know that's really about all you need.

But still, I wasn't hardly ready for it. "No!"

Daddy nodded like a deacon. "Least that's what I thought I saw."

Daddy took me to church sometimes—Momma's church,

the Church of the Cross—whenever we were in town on Sundays. It was Episcopal and kinda snooty, but I still knew about Noah's ark and Moses parting the waters and Jesus walking upon deep blue Galilee. "Like Jesus?" I asked.

"Yep, bub, just like Jesus, one foot right in front of the other."

And then I laid back down and got comfortable as I could and Daddy laid his hand on my knee and he told me this story and I will tell it to you as close as I can.

Daddy had driven into town, swapped the pickup for his squad car and picked up Jim Bodine. Bodine was Daddy's deputy. He was nice to little white boys like me and, very privately, to pretty colored gals like Miss Evie. He would slip over and see her once a week, or so, and he was pretty tolerable for the next couple of days. Otherwise, you'd have swore he ate shingle nails for breakfast. Daddy kind of inherited Bodine when he got the job and he put up with him til Dr. Indigo—well, I'm getting ahead of myself again.

Anyway, Daddy and Bodine drove on down to Savannah and got on the Waving Girl at the end of River Street. The Waving Girl was a side-wheel steamer, pine planked, about a hundred and twenty feet at the waterline. She was named after the lonely sister of the keeper of the Elba Island Light, way out in the Savannah River channel. She was seduced by a sailor—the story goes—who solemnly swore he'd come back in a marrying mood. So she met every incoming ship—a flag by day and a lantern by night—for the next forty years. The Waving

Girl—the boat, not that lonesome woman—huffed up from Savannah twice a week, carrying groceries and mail to the islands that didn't have bridges.

The Savannah police had their eye on the Waving Girl for a couple of months. Sugar was hard to get because of the war, but there was always sacks and sacks going over to Williman. Savannah is Georgia but Williman is in Calhoun County, so when they saw rolls of copper tubing and cases of Mason jars going aboard, they called Daddy.

Daddy said they were about halfway through Field's Cut when there came a great whooping and hollering from the passengers and deckhands. Way out over the salt marsh, Jesus was walking on the water. Fifty Negroes rushed the starboard rail and the boat heeled and freight slid and Daddy thought for sure she'd roll slap upside down. The Capum started cussing and got out his glass and hollered it wasn't Jesus at all, but somebody he called The Doctor. That sent the Negroes to the other rail and the freight after them and it's a God's wonder Waving Girl didn't roll that way, too.

I knew better than to interrupt Daddy when he got working a story, but I couldn't help myself. "What kind of a doctor?"

Daddy paused and considered. "Well, he was all up in white. He didn't look like no professor. He weren't no medical doctor and I don't reckon he was a veterinarian either."

"Well, what you reckon?"

Daddy paused again. "I can't reckon," he said, "but I reckon I'm gonna find out."

I knew he would. Way out over the Little Glory, heat lightning flickered and rolled where the bright sky met the darker lines of trees. The wind smelt of rain and it moaned through the window screens sweet and soft and low, a-whoo, a-whoo, like doves when they roost on a hot summer evening.

I had a million questions and I figured to ask half of them before I'd let him out of the room. But I never got the chance. There was more of the story coming.

By and by the Waving Girl got around the bend and the passengers settled some and sat amidships in nervous little knots, and the crew got the freight lashed down in case they saw anybody else walking on the water.

They made Williman Landing along about two. Back in those days there'd be a celebration when the Savannah boat came in. Just about the whole island was there, all dressed up like they were expecting Franklin Delano Roosevelt to come rolling down the gangway. The kettles steaming up shrimp and crabs and sometimes oysters, little kids peeking round their mommas' dresses, and all the young bucks trying to make time with the girls. And the Model As, the Model Ts, and mules and oxcarts backed down to the landing to take on groceries and mail, but especially the sugar.

That was back before every boat had a radio. Those old steamers had a whistle code—a short blast for a port passing, two for starboard, a long blast before casting off, and three to clear the dock and make ready to take lines. But when the Waving Girl was two hundred yards out in the channel, somebody pulled the whistle four times.

Up on the dock, there was a flinging down of food, a flying

off of hats and caps, and a great billowing of denim and calico as every man, woman and child on Williman Island headed for the hill. Daddy said the dust hung in the air for a full ten minutes afterwards.

Daddy heard those four blasts, Bodine heard it, so did everybody on deck, and that gang of Negroes on the end of the dock damn sure heard it, too. But the Capum swore up and down he only blew three and the mate backed him up and nobody on the deck remembered a single thing, no water walker, no whistle, no nothing. And the folks on the hill? Daddy couldn't find a one of them.

No, he found two. One was Bo Manigault, who looked for all the world like a New York Negro but wasn't. The other was that damn Cuffee Wiggins, the man whose name Harley Davidson said he forgot.

You know, the Good Book says all things work for good for those who love the Lord. I reckon it's true, but it's sure hard to see sometimes. It's a tangled up mess, as I can figure it. Trifling things mean a lot and huge things come to nothing. If you could go back and change one sorry-ass little detail from thirty years ago, you might be a lot better off today. Or you might be dead.

I ain't dead yet, but I'm getting up there and sometimes I get off on a tangent. I was talking about when I was nine years old and didn't get to go fishing 'cause Daddy had to run off chasing a bootlegger. And how I was laying in bed and the heat lightning was flashing and the thunder starting to grumble way off to the west and daddy was trying to make up for being gone by telling me all of this. This business of Bo Manigault coming to pick up a crate of chickens. And Cuffey Wiggins' foot sticking out from beneath a stack of palmetto fronds and how those little things changed everything.

Course, Bodine was all over Bo Manigault in a second. Well, why not? Here you got a black man in a purple suit driving a four door Packard and picking up a crate of chickens. "Where you goin' with them chickens, boy?" was a dead cinch, specially with Bodine.

But that Bo Manigault wouldn't kiss Bodine's fanny, no sir. "These Savannah chickens," he said, "Won't no other kind do."

Bodine had ridden the boat over with those chickens and he damn sure knew where they come from. He wanted to know where they was going. Bo started to sass him again and Bodine would have put the billy stick to him if Daddy hadn't stopped him. Daddy couldn't see nothing illegal in a man in a thousand dollar car and a hundred dollar suit toting chickens. And he wasn't about to see someone's head get split over it.

So they turned Bo Manigault loose and he went off with his chickens and Daddy and Bodine walked. They walked past fields and little shanties, past swamps and sloughs and gator wallows and acres upon acres of deep green woods. They walked two and a half miles down a rutted sandy road and they did not see another living soul.

But then Daddy, who could read the ground like a Choctaw, found a trail through the woods, too broad for deer and too tall for hogs. There, at the end of the trail, he found the still.

He said it was as good as local stills get: a half dozen barrels of stinking corn mash, a twenty gallon copper boiler—double-lapped so the lead solder wouldn't get to you and drive you blind—a hank of good tubing for the condenser, and upwards of a hundred Mason jars. The thing was powered by palmetto fronds, which burn hot and quick and make no smoke. There was a pile of them there and a foot sticking out from beneath the pile.

And the foot was connected to a man.

I was wide awake again. I hollered "The Doctor!"

"No, son, it wasn't the doctor."

"Did you get him?"

Daddy nodded. "We had us a little foot race and a wrastling match."

"Where's he now?"

Daddy smiled and patted my leg and began to sing, slow and soft as any lullaby, a song he heard on the radio:

He's in the jailhouse now.
He's in the jailhouse now.
I told him once, I told him twice,
Quit dealin' cards and rollin' dice.
He's in the jailhouse now.

I laughed and Daddy laughed and I loved him so. Then he walked to the window and looked out at the pewtery moonlight and the gathering thunderheads. The first blue bolt lit the lines in his face. "I'll shut this window," he said. "It's going to blow here directly."

"Daddy?"

"What, bub?"

"What you gonna do to him?"

Daddy was watching the storm roll in. Knowing what I know now, I can tell you he was still a little boogered by the water walker. "Who?" he said.

"The bootlegger."

"Oh, I don't know. The judge will probably send him off to the penitentiary. We gonna try him on Wednesday."

I was up off the pillow again. "Can I come?"

Daddy looked at me like I was a mule he was getting ready to buy. "Well, we'll see."

"Can I bring Harley Davidson?"

Daddy shook his head. "I said we'll see."

Chapter Four

The Little Glory River works its way east from the Coosawhatchie Swamp, twisting through the cypress and tupelo and soft maple in broad sweeping bends, turning at times nearly back upon itself. It's fresh in its upper reaches, with water the color of good strong coffee, a tincture of needle and leaf and rotting logs. The river runs brown and brackish past the sad old rice fields of Big Glory and Little Glory, past Bluff and Brickyard and Airy Hall plantations, and finally blue and saline as it slows and spreads and meets the wrinkling sea.

There, on its last great bend before deep blue water, is a high bluff and upon that bluff is the town of Albemarle, South Carolina, named for George, some duke of the same name, good friend of King Charles II.

Albemarle was to be a great port city, the New London of the New World, where English ships were to bring English rifles and axes and plows and load up with Carolina indigo and rice and cotton. But Charleston and Savannah became the ports and Albemarle languished, a den of smugglers and pirates who drank and whored at waterside public houses, their longboats tied out back for convenient escape.

About 1820, Albemarle was discovered by the local gentry seeking refuge from the heat and mosquitoes and malaria of inland plantations. They built great houses along the bluff, with high ceilings, broad verandas, large windows to catch the sea breeze, and backyard gardens all rustling with magnolia, camellia, and oleander. My distant cousin William Grayson, who took it upon himself to write a long and overly literary retort to *Uncle Tom's Cabin*, said this about Albemarle's early citizens: "They were a generous but somewhat rough race, much addicted to fishing, drinking, and practical joking. They met monthly to hunt and dine, and from these festivals no man was permitted to go home sober."

The damn Yankees put an end to all this—not General Sherman as you might expect, but Flag Officer Samuel Dupont, who shot his way past the Confederate forts on November 3, 1861. The locals had cleared out the previous Sunday, when the arrival of the enemy was announced from the pulpit at the Church of the Cross. Ol Massa gone away, great throngs of field hands descended upon the mansions, put on fine European clothes and waltzed outrageously and ate and fornicated and busted up furniture til the whiskey ran out. When the Marines got to Albemarle a month later, they found streets paved with broken glass, doors and gates swinging on the wind, pigs inside on the Oriental carpets, and only two white men remaining. One was from New York and figured he did not have to leave. The other was so drunk, he could not leave.

The Yankees didn't burn Albemarle, but they sure were hard

on it. They pulled up Church of the Cross tombstones and used them for operating tables right there in the sanctuary. They buried sawed off arms and legs out in the graveyard and whole corpses too, so now if you try to bury your granddaddy out there, you'll dig up more men than you'll plant.

The Yankees set their generals and colonels and captains up in the mansions and stabled their horses in the Calhoun County Courthouse, where eighty-odd years later, on a bright morning getting on towards the end of May, Harley Davidson and I sat in the shade below the statue of General Wade Hampton.

It was a fine bronze statue, all green from the sea air and spattered by the local pigeons. Old Marse Wade upon his charger, with bristling beard and upraised sword, like he was about to lop the head right off somebody from New Jersey.

Wade Hampton was a rich planter from the red clay country who outfitted a whole Confederate brigade out of his own pocket and was the first man to whip George Armstrong Custer in a cavalry fight. The second was Crazy Horse. After the war, he took the state back from the Republican carpetbaggers and rode to the governor's mansion with a pistol-packing gang of his former troopers. The Negroes, unprotected now by Yankee bayonets, were quick to swap sides and have been voting Democrat ever since.

We were sitting there when Bodine rattled up in the paddy wagon. I call it a paddy wagon, but it was just a flatbed truck with a cage on the back, like what you'd use to haul hounds out to a deer drive, only a little taller so a man had room to sit on a little board bench. And in the cage was a man in handcuffs and a striped suit. It was Cuffey Wiggins, the Williman Island bootlegger, on his way to state pen hard time. Or, more likely, hard labor, the chain gang, digging ditches, grubbing brush, or picking up white people's trash alongside the road.

Like Daddy, this Cuffey Wiggins wasn't much to look at, skinny and shaky and yellow eyed, like he'd been testing too much of his own product. Being in jail a couple of days probably didn't help, and neither did the ride from the jail to the courthouse. It was only three blocks, but Bodine never went from here to there, specially with a colored prisoner, which most of them were. He'd take them on a little tour of Ward 6, the interior streets of Albemarle, a jungle of kudzu and wisteria, a hodgepodge of careening unpainted shanties, beer joints, pool halls, and whore houses, acres of sad and rusting wrecks of buggies, wagons, and cars. Bodine would blow his horn as he drove his prisoner through those rutted streets, and would make another round if he could gather a crowd. And then there was the walk from the paddy wagon to the courthouse, drug along by the cuffs, a good general cussing, and a cadence kept with a nightstick.

I'd seen it a couple of times, but Harley Davidson hadn't, so he said: "What's wrong with you white people?"

It was the first time Harley Davidson lumped me up with all the other buckra so I didn't know just what to say. I mean, we ate the same food, talked the same way, lived on the same patch of ground. He might have been black and I might have been white, but from a hundred feet, me all tan from days in

31

the creek, and him all tan from his high-yaller daddy, you wouldn't see much difference at all. Up close you'd see his eyes were brown and mine were blue and his hair was a lot curlier and that was about it.

"I mean you-all got ever-thang. Why ain't you happy?"

I figured I was happy enough and I told him so. I mean, I missed my momma and I didn't see Daddy much, but I had Miss Althea's cooking and the run of Little Glory.

"No, Mr. Lil Mac, I ain't talkin' 'bout you, I'm talkin' 'bout all you white people. You ever hear of a nigger jumping off a bridge?"

"Why no, I guess not."

"Or killing hisself jumping out a window? A nigger might get drunk and fall off his porch..."

This was getting too much for me. I was figuring hard to come up with something, but the only thing that come to me was the time Harley Davidson almost drowned trying to retrieve the cast net I let get away from me. I stuck one end of the oar in the water and he had scrambled up it like a cat. "Well, if you so damn perfect, why can't you swim?"

Harley Davidson looked at me like I was the dumbest living thing in the world. "Swim? Why Mr. Lil Mac, what's wrong with you? You know we bones is way too heavy. Just you try being a nigger sometimes."

Well, that stumped me, so I let it drop.

We followed Bodine and poor old Cuffey Wiggins up the sidewalk, up the stairs, and through the great oak swinging doors into the cool dark of the halls of justice.

The place was packed, white folks to one side, colored on the other. Half of Williman Island must have been there, fat old women, skinny old women, young women fat and skinny and in between, men of all shapes and sizes, children of various ages, every last one of them dressed their best. There was an American flag up front, our sweet blue state flag with its lovely crescent moon and palmetto tree, and then the bold crossbuck of the old Confederacy. There was also a picture of Moses, looking about like Wade Hampton in his pajamas, handing the Ten Commandments to the Children of Israel, all dressed in pajamas, too, and finally that old bastard John C. Calhoun, whose ideas brought Sherman down upon us all, looking like he just tried to pass gas and had let a little more slip out.

Harley and me sat down separate and the bailiff sung out and the judge came out from his chambers, his robe unbuttoned and flapping in the breeze he made.

This was back before they gave poor folks free lawyers, back when *habeas corpus* was a funny term in a dead language, when "innocent until proven guilty" was a polite sarcasm. The court believed in the cops and if the sheriff went to the trouble to arrest a man, he must be guilty. So the solicitor read the charges and they called up Cuffey and hauled out a Bible and made him lay his hand upon it and swear to God he would tell the truth. They asked him his name and he told the truth. They asked him if he had ever been in this court before and he said no.

"Cuffey Wiggins," the solicitor thumbed a stack of papers and gravely asked, "what about July 13, 1936? What about August 4, 1940?"

Cuffey got all twiss-mout, as we say down here, working his lips and screwing up his face and running his tongue over his gums. Then he smiled broadly. "Oh, nawsuh, that be in the cote-room down the hall."

There was much laughing and amening and leg slapping from the colored side and the judge's hammer came down. "Order in this court!" he shouted. "One more outburst like that and I'll clear the court and try Cuffey Wiggins in private!"

That settled them down some. Next, they asked Cuffey if he made bad likker and he said no. Then the solicitor came up with a Mason jar gave it to the judge who sniffed it and sipped it and pronounced it good. The solicitor asked it be admitted into evidence as good likker, since the court had found it so. The judge agreed and they labeled it "Exhibit A Good Likker" and put it on the corner of the bench where the judge kept a sharp eye on it for the rest of the proceedings. So Cuffey had admitted, in the judicial standards of the day, to making good whiskey. They sent him back to his seat and called Daddy.

Daddy sure looked good up there, slicked down hair and shined up shoes and pressed pants and a clean khaki shirt with the gold-plated star that told the world he was Sheriff of Calhoun County. Lordy, was I proud. The solicitor made a little joke about swearing in or not swearing in and how Daddy would tell the truth, no matter what. Daddy grinned and said, sure, of course, and so on.

Well, there's the truth, the whole truth, and nothing but the truth and two out of three ain't bad. Daddy told the truth and nothing but the truth, the story pretty much like he told me when I was laying in bed and the storm was building off beyond the Little Glory treeline. All about the trail and the still and the foot sticking out from beneath the palmettoes and even the foot race and the wrastling match. But he didn't tell the whole truth and I guess that's OK, since they didn't ask him. Not a word about the four blasts on the boat whistle, the stampede up into the woods, or the man walking on the water like Jesus.

The clerk took all that down and they turned Daddy loose and hauled up some shiftless Negro named Jonathan Polite who they caught with a jar of Cuffey Wiggins' shine down in Cedar Grove, a little swamp hamlet just across the line from Savannah. Now, if Cuffey was wasted from hanging his lip over too much of his own stuff, Jonathan Polite was worse—bow-legged, knobby at knee and elbow, shaky, wild-eyed, dirty, ragged, and maybe even a little drunk. He had been in jail as a material witness, but material witnesses sometimes needed material and Bodine sometimes slipped them some, if Daddy wasn't around.

They were well into the formalities when I heard the court-room door swish open. Well, maybe I didn't hear it. But somebody did and said under his breath, "Oh Lord, here come the doctor."

I turned and there he was, Dr. Indigo. Well, I didn't know his name then, but I sure would later. He was all up in quality black and looked for all the world like a retired undertaker or a bishop in the AME church, tall, lean, wise, but there were a couple of peculiar things about him. He was wearing blue sunglasses and carrying a snake-head cane.

Dr. Indigo eased his way up the aisle, thump, thump, working the floor with his cane with every step, and the whispering washed through the colored side like little waves on a low tide sandbar. There wasn't really any place to sit, but when Dr. Indigo chose a bench they found him plenty of room, folks damn near sitting atop one another until there was five feet of empty bench on either side.

Now Daddy and Bodine and the judge and the solicitor were all busy with Jonathan Polite and the interrogation went something like this:

"Jonathan, is this your good whiskey?"

"No suh!"

"Jonathan, are you sure?"

There was a long silence, then Jonathan Polite said, "Well suh, maybe it was til the po-leece took 'em."

"OK, Jonathan, do you testify that you were once in possession of this jar of good whiskey?"

Another long silence. "Well, suh, I don't rightly know. All them likker jars look alike to me."

Then the solicitor changed tacks and said, "Yes Jonathan, we understand that you cannot specifically identify this jar of good whiskey as yours, but will you testify that you did once possess a similar jar of good whiskey and that it was taken from you by Deputy Jim Bodine?"

That was one hell of a question to ask Jonathan Polite. Maybe he understood it, maybe he didn't, but either way, he never got the chance to answer 'cause that's about when he saw

Dr. Indigo staring at him. Jonathan Polite looked and I looked and there the doctor sat, chewing like he was working a big plug of Brown's Mule, long rivulets of juice running down his chin, drip, dripping onto the courthouse floor, still scarred from the shoes of Yankee horses.

If Jonathan Polite was scared before, now he was—as the Good Book says—sore afraid.

He did not answer.

So the solicitor turned to the judge and said, "Your honor, we can call Deputy Bodine who will testify that this indeed is the jar of good whiskey he took from Jonathan Polite."

And the judge said, "No need to bother. I will order the clerk to enter a positive response to that question."

The solicitor smiled, nodded, and turned back to Jonathan Polite. "Now, Jonathan, the court has found that you were once in possession of this jar of good whiskey. Now can you tell the court where you got it?"

Doctor Indigo kept chewing and drooling. Jonathan Polite worked his lips, but no sound came out.

"Jonathan, there is no need to be afraid. Just tell the judge what you told Sheriff McCloud after your arrest."

You could have heard a fly buzz. The whole crowd, the colored side anyway, leaned forward to catch the answer.

But there was no answer.

So the judge sternly said. "Jonathan Polite, if you refuse to answer this time, I will send you back to jail until you do."

The solicitor jumped in again. "Let me refresh your memory." He picked up a stack of papers and began to read. "On

May 2, 1942, you told Sheriff Mac McCloud you purchased this jar of good whiskey from the defendant, Cuffey Wiggins. Is that correct?"

By now, Jonathan Polite was shaking and rubbing his arms and the backs of his hands like they was covered with red ants, and even from way back where I was sitting, I could see little drops of spit at the corners of his mouth. When he finally spoke there were no words, just a long low groan like the last growl from a dying dog. And then Jonathan Polite clutched his throat and pitched headlong out of the witness box, thrashing and kicking on the floor like he'd just been struck by lightning.

A great hullabaloo broke loose among the spectators, Hallelujah and Praise God and Do Jesuses like it was the Reverend Billy Kinkaid's Miracle Holy Ghost Soul Saving Revival instead of court.

The judge was hammering away and nobody was paying him any mind at all and the bailiff was shouting, "Get a doctor! Get a doctor!"

And that's when I heard Harley Davidson sing out, "Hot damn, Mr. Lil Mac, we gots all the doctor we need!"

Chapter Five

Daddy caught particular hell about losing that case. He did not actually lose it, but I already told you how the court trusted the law to arrest only guilty men and if somehow somebody accidentally went free, it must have been the sheriff's fault. On Wednesday afternoon he had visits from representatives of the Women's Christian Temperance Union, the Naomi Circle of the First Albemarle Methodist Church, The Loyal Daughters of Confederate Veterans, and from The Holy Sisters of I Shall Arise On That Glorious Getting Up Morning, who blew into his office in full battle dress, puffy and hopeless white matrons with skirts a-billowing and little badges that read *Lips That Touch Wine Will Never Touch Mine* with the little red, white, and blue ribbons fluttering from their considerable breath. By Thursday he was wishing he would have taken me after those puppy drum rather than gone chasing a bootlegger.

Friday, things died down a bit. We stayed on the plantation Saturday and laid out of church on Sunday, but early Monday morning, the *Palmetto Post* hit the stands and it started all over again.

Daddy called it the *Weekly Wipe*. It wasn't much of a

paper—normally just the Savannah boat schedule, the tide tables, a bunch of ads for tooth whitener, stove black, and cough medicine, society news about Miss So-and-So having coffee at her maiden aunt's and who got married, baptized, or buried, incomprehensible notices from swindling lawyers trying to steal some poor colored man's land. Of course, that year there was a bunch of war news and a list of dead or wounded at the bottom of page three.

The editor, Old Man Will Mahoney, would take his patriotism with sour mash whiskey and turn out headlines like: "Flat-face Japs Die on Wake Island," "Coward Italians Run Everywhere," and "Damn Hitler Invades Denmark and Norway."

That last one had me pretty worried for awhile. Denmark and Norway were two little farm towns about four hours away, settled by Scandinavian immigrants in the 1840s and I expected Damn Hitler to come rolling into Albemarle any minute, standing in the back of a black German car with his chest puffed up and his hand out like he was about to take a swat at one of those big green horse flies that torment us every summer. I asked Daddy if he and Bodine would deputize a bunch of citizens and try to cut him off at the Port Royal ferry, but Daddy laughed and explained that there were two Denmarks and two Norways and the ones Hitler was bothering were clean on the other side of the sea.

But the headlines that last Monday in May blew the war news right off the front page. It said "Notorious Bootlegger Goes Free."

That was the day we were finally going to get after those puppy drum. It was Decoration Day, of course, when the Negroes turned out in throngs to honor the Yankees who had set them free. White folks celebrated separately, on Confederate Memorial Day, drawling soft speeches and drinking iced tea and eating deviled eggs and those little crust-cut-off sandwiches beneath the great rustling oaks in the Confederate section of the National Cemetery on Boundary Street.

But on Yankee Memorial Day—Decoration Day—the Negroes busted loose with singing and dancing and a brass band parade going down Bay Street to the Little Glory River where they dumped extravagant garlands overboard to remember the nine Yankee sailors who had died getting past the rebel forts. There was a carnival with a Ferris wheel and merry-go-round and a genuine steam calliope, and all along Boundary Street the flags fluttered and little board and tarpaper stands sold everything from fried chicken to fried mullet and boiled corn and parched peanuts and the white folks stayed home.

I went down to the creek again and corralled some more fiddlers and threw the net for shrimp and finger mullet, in case we got into the spottail bass. We drove into town and Daddy stopped by the office to take care of a few things and gave me two dollars and sent me downtown to Billy Rhett's Hardware for extra rigs in case we lost a few on the oyster shell rakes like we generally did.

Billy Rhett's Coastal Carolina Hardware was one of those long-gone and magic places, smelling of dust and rope and kerosene and fish meal fertilizer, with cast nets and oars and oarlocks hung on the walls, and the marvelous barrels of nails of all sizes and bulging bundles of cedar shakes in the dark corners and in the middle of it all, glorious bins of corn and butter-beans and beet seed for the big Negro gardens, and shining rolls of fencing to keep out the free roaming cattle and wild island ponies.

Billy Rhett had a pedigree most like mine. His great, great grandfather had led the Colonial Naval Militia against old Stede Bonnet, the Barbadian gentleman who took up piracy to get away from a nagging wife. Like the Heywards, the Rhetts was about whittled down to nothing. The name even got lost, when the last of the Rhett daughters married a Smith. But one Christmas morning, R. B. Smith and his three brothers descended the stairs to announce a gift to their mother. They would change their name to Rhett. Nobody remembers what their daddy said, but Robert Barnwell Rhett grew up and got himself elected U.S. Senator and did all he could to rile the Yankees into burning us out. And eighty years later, there was Billy, ten years older than Daddy, running a hardware store in Albemarle instead of being governor.

Billy Rhett held onto hope of better times by smoking Cuban seegars and wearing a white suit. Whenever he wore some other color, he broke out in hives, so he told everybody he was allergic to dye. A man in a white suit couldn't hardly be expected to hump freight and rub up against cans of roofing tar, so Billy Rhett built himself a tower right above the fishing tackle, and he would sit up there with the phone and the receipt book and the cash register and lip that seegar and beller out commands to a tribe of Negroes who ran and got you what you wanted. There was a confusion of commerce most days and later on I learned to call in what I needed. The phone come first, he figured, 'cause you might get disgusted if it rang too long and hang up, but once you were in the store, he figured you'd wait.

But the fishing tackle was right there where I could lay hands on it, so I picked out a half dozen rigs and some four once teardrop sinkers what wouldn't get hung up bad as the pyramid ones. I come on back to the office and walked right into the latest round of public outrage.

I could hear the hollering way out in the street. Bodine yelling he was the chief deputy and would handle any more complaints and then somebody said, "Hell, you're the only deputy!" and then another man cussing the first man for cussing. I didn't want to miss a minute of it, so I threw the tackle into the pickup and ducked inside.

There was Daddy sitting at his desk fiddling with a little cloth bag about the size and color of a peach pit, trying to hard ignore the fracas on the other side of the desk. One of the men was Rauls, and for the life of me I can't remember his first name. He ran Sea Island Taxi Service. The other man was waving a copy of the *Palmetto Post*. I didn't know him, but found out soon enough he was the Reverend Billy Kinkaid, himself, the famous tent evangelist who I heard about on the radio when I was waiting for Daddy to take me fishing that day we did not go.

The Reverend Billy Kinkaid could make otherwise normal people bust loose in Latin and Greek and ancient Hebrew. He could make the deaf hear, the dumb speak, and the lame rise up and dance. Daddy said when Billy Kinkaid pulled stakes and moved to another town, they'd be a truckload of crutches and wheelchairs left behind. The Negroes would paw through the pile, busting up the crutches for kindling and making dog carts and barrows and wagons from the wheelchairs for trundling groceries home from the store or crabs and oysters up from the creek.

The men kept up their hollering and Daddy kept messing with that little bag, picking at the stitching with the point of his Barlow jackknife.

I'd seen that bag before. When the Negroes had come a-boiling out of court, laughing and yelling and pushing Cuffey Wiggins before them like he had just broke the four minute mile, Old Doctor Indigo had walked up to Daddy and, without a word, put the little bag in his hand. Daddy slipped it into his pocket, and now he was trying to figure out what in the hell it was.

Finally, Daddy had enough. He looked up at Rauls and said something like this: "Mr. Rauls, I've heard there are two types of people who want bootleggers in jail. Preachers and other bootleggers."

Rauls looked like he had just swallowed a frog. "Why Mac, you ain't accusing me?"

Bodine got this big grin and Daddy said, "No, when I accuse you, I will come with a warrant. But I have noticed a lot of coming and going around the back of your cab stand."

Then the Reverend Billy Kinkaid cut in. "Thy shall not bear false witness against thy neighbor."

Daddy said, "You know your book, Reverend. You remember what Jesus said about the Last Days?"

The Reverend's face lit up. "And I seen the City of God coming down out of the heavens!"

Bodine, who got religion once or twice a year, said, "There'll be weeping and wailing and snatching out of teeth."

"That's *gnashing*, Brother Bodine."

"Yeah," Bodine said, "gnashing out of teeth."

Daddy got the bag open and poured a thimble of white powder out upon his desk. A little catspaw of breeze eased through the window and caught some of it, moved it around like loose sand on a windy beach. Daddy scraped it up into an envelope, but got some of it on his fingers.

Daddy kept talking while he worked. "Jesus says 'whatever is whispered in private will be shouted from the rooftops'."

Then the Reverend got all puffed up. "You mean you see yourself as an instrument of the Lord?"

"No," Daddy said, "just an instrument of the law. And I'm just asking questions. That's my job." Then he turned to Bodine and held out the envelope. "Send this to the lab in Columbia. I want to know what it is."

"It's dope," Bodine said. "Nigger devil dust."

"Why in the world," Daddy asked, "would an old colored man give a sheriff dope right in the court of law?"

"Why would a nigger witness...."

Daddy cut him off. "Bodine, you know I don't like that word."

"'Scuse me, Mac." Then Bodine bucked up real sarcastic.

"Why would one of our drunk *darker brethren* have a slobbering fit right in the middle of testimony that would send another one of our *darker brethren* bootleggers to jail? Hell, Mac, none of this makes sense!"

"It don't make sense to me, either," Daddy said. "But somehow I'm gonna figure it out." Then he turned to Rauls and the Reverend Billy Kinkaid. "Does that suit you gentlemen?"

Rauls and the Reverend nodded, standing there, their bare faces hanging out.

Well, we got to go fishing that day. Sort of. I should have known something was up 'cause Daddy took the squad car and county boat and Bodine, too.

That's the way it was in those days. The sheriff was the law. If Daddy wanted a ditch cleaned on the plantation, or brush cut along the drive, or the potholes filled with oyster shells Bodine would haul out the chain gang. If there wasn't any chain gang, and most of the time there wasn't, Bodine would go prowling around Ward Six, arresting gamblers and drunks and lay-abouts and pretty soon we'd have us one. And if we wanted to go fishing, Daddy could use the county boat all day long if he could figure ten minutes of county business into the deal.

The county boat wasn't much—a twenty-foot skiff—a bateau, we called it. Bateau is French for boat and how we got that name is a mystery to me. I've lived sixty-odd years in these parts and I haven't run into a Frenchman yet, but I guess that don't really matter. Anyway, she was five-quarter cypress, heavy as all get out, and you had to bail like hell until the water got to the planking and swole the seams shut. But it had a rickety trailer made from Model A Ford parts and it had an outboard motor, an old six horse Elgin, as cantankerous a piece of machinery as you'll ever find, and a pelican could pass you flying upwind. But even if you had to lay up for a hour and file the points and clean the plugs, it sure beat rowing.

Bodine hitched the trailer to the squad car, Daddy gassed the old Elgin, I fetched the rigs and the tackle and the bait and the sandwiches from the pickup and piled everything, me included, into the back of the squad car. We pulled out of the jail yard, drove down Scot Street, turned east on Bay and ran slap dab into the middle of the Decoration Day parade.

They come a whooping around the corner, five hundred strong, led by our union of domestic help, the Eleanor Roosevelt No Stoop No Reach Club, followed up by the Robert Smalls High School marching band, which found two beats where a white band would only find one.

Robert Smalls had been dead thirty years, but he still was a great hero to the Negroes. He was born a slave, the son of his master and the big house cook. As you might expect, his mistress took a dim view of his parentage, and treated him poorly, until he saved one of his half brothers when he fell overboard crabbing in Niggerhead Cut, which Bodine called Colored Cranium Creek just to spite Daddy. When Robert Smalls' master died, his mistress sold all the slaves but him and took him and the children to live in a town house in Charleston.

In Charleston, Robert Smalls went to work as a deckhand on a riverboat and gave his mistress half his wages. The other half he saved so he could someday buy his freedom, a price his mistress set at seven hundred dollars. In a couple of years he had worked his way up into the wheel house and gained quite a reputation as a pilot. He had just about raised the money when the war broke out and he was pressed into piloting a Confederate gunboat. A year later, the captain ashore drunk, Robert Smalls loaded up a dozen slaves and steamed out and turned the gunboat over to the Yankee fleet. Abe Lincoln set him free, gave him half the value of the boat as a reward, and Robert Smalls went back to Albemarle and bought the house where he was once a slave. After the war, his mistress came back to town and he moved her into her old bedroom and took care of her for the rest of her days. He got elected to Congress and served four terms and did what he could to keep the red-necks—the poor buckra—from bothering his people. I know I'm getting off track again, but I wanted to tell you this so you'd know things down here are not as simple as you might think.

Anyway, there was me and Daddy and Bodine stuck in Albemarle's yearly traffic jam, Decoration Day 1942, the Robert Smalls High School Band strutting and the majorettes moving in marvelous ways no white gal could ever match. Then came the sisters from the First Union African Baptist, with hats like square riggers under full sail, all up in white and purple and greens that shone in the morning sun like the light off a drake mallard's head and behind them two dozen children bearing bouquets of flowers to throw upon the waters of the Little Glory and, finally, a long parade of dilapidated cars, pickups, farm trucks and flatbeds, some clattering and steaming, all loaded to capacity with jubilant Negroes, and festooned with

red, white and blue bunting and signs quoting The Battle
Hymn of the Republic: Glory Hallelujah, Mine Eyes Have Seen
the Glory, and Trampling out the Vintage, which I did not
understand and I doubt if anybody in that crowd did, either.

Bodine sat in the passenger seat, chomping a cigar, mumbling to himself, singling out various Negroes for specific deri-
sion and casting general disparagements upon the race as a
whole. And then he cussed a cuss so bad I will not tell you what
it was. I looked and there was a white Packard touring car, with
those suicide doors, you know what I mean, those that will
open backwards and throw you out onto the highway if you
lean on the handle wrong. A banner along the running board
read He Restoreth My Soul. Behind the wheel was a Negro in a
purple suit. And cuddled up next to him was a high-yaller gal
in a white dress, Miss Evie, herself.

Now, I seen some good looking colored gals in my time:
high-stepping majorettes in the Robert Smalls High School
Marching Band, all brown and slick and jiggling; pretty black
whores waiting for dates on Savannah street corners that kept
the body shops busy from the wrecks they caused; and this
waitress I met years later down in the New Orleans French
Quarter who I could tell you about but I won't. But I never
seen nothing like that Miss Evie.

Lordy, she was a looker. I was only nine years old, but that
didn't matter. She was long-legged and well put together and
about the color of coffee when you dump too much milk in it.
Her hair was piled on top of her head, all wove up in braids like
a sweetgrass basket, and when she smiled her teeth flashed like

the chrome on that Packard car. You couldn't hardly blame Bodine for slipping over to see her when nobody was looking.

Bodine bit off the end of his cigar and the rest of it fell into his lap and burnt a hole in his britches. He opened the door and leapt out and took off his hat and threw it onto the pavement and jumped up and down on it, cussing a blue streak.

The Negro in the purple suit leaned out the window and grinned and said, "Lawd, watch that white man dance."

You could hear the Negroes hooting and hollering all up and down Bay Street. But Miss Evie just sat there like the queen of the Sudan. And she did not say a thing.

Chapter Six

The river lay before us, blue, wide, and wonderful—the Little Glory—nearing the sea and now thoroughly salt. We hummed along, the Elgin laying a fine line of blue smoke. Bodine ran the motor, Daddy sat amidships and I was in the forward seat, my legs dangling over the side, the green bow wave snatching at my toes. The tide, an hour into full flood, swirled beneath us and the motor labored and the bateau skittered like a car with bald tires on a rainslick road.

We passed the old tabby fort on Palmetto Bluff, all grown up with oaks older than anybody's granddaddy, past Spanish Wells where the galleons took on water in Columbus' time, past hummocks and islands and marsh the color of ripening wheat. And then there was one more bend in the river and way out beyond the bell buoys, the wrinkling sea.

I could never see it without thanking God I was born here and not in Kansas or Alberta where half the landscape is clouds and sky and the wind moves grass, not water. The tall pines on the headlands and the beaches shining like yellow ribbons and the sea birds wheeling and the surf rumbling, though I could not hear it over the whining Elgin. Miss Althea, born and grown up and almost old on the black headwaters of the Little Glory, had never seen it at all. One September afternoon, Daddy and I took her down to Capers Island. She made the chicken and the deviled eggs and the sweet iced tea and laid the basket upon the pickup tailgate and struggled up the dune and stood at the top, hands on her hips, considering the broad beach, the gnarled driftwood and great blue expanse beyond. Then she turned to me and said, "What you mean, boy? That ain't so big."

But it was big. Damn big.

Daddy had his eye on a shell rake just inside the surf line at Grenadier Shoals. The shoals broke the big ocean rollers and made a half mile of slick water there on the landward side and oysters had taken root upon what was left of the steamship Lawrence. The Lawrence was out of Philadelphia, bound for Savannah, when the '93 Storm shoved her up onto the shoals. The passengers and crew lashed themselves to the rigging and rode out the storm and went ashore the next morning at daybreak, rowing two lifeboats right up into the Hunting Island woods, the water was still so high. The next couple of storms broke her up until there was nothing left but her firebox and boiler and her bottom, and by the time I was a boy, if you didn't know the story, you wouldn't know there was a ship there at all. The jumble of shells upon shells grew seaweed and soft coral and sponges and held crustaceans, water bugs, and little fish and when the flood tide rushed over all of it, bigger fish came to feed.

Bodine idled down and swung the bateau uptide and then killed the motor and Daddy eased the anchor over the side and let out line and we bobbed and swung back until it was an easy cast to the edge of the shells. It was a magic time, fishing with Daddy while the surf mumbled and the sun ricocheted off the ocean swells and the wind sang sad songs of Cape Lookout, Cape Hatteras, and beyond. It even got to working on old Bodine, only two hours off a hat stomping fit. His face softened and lightened til it was about two shades off pink. He even baited up my hook and helped me unsnarl a couple of backlashes. You know, a man just can't worry and fish at the same time.

Now, I don't know what's wrong with me, jumping into that fishing story like that. I never told you about Daddy's blue sunglasses or about meeting Miss Marzette, either. And if I left that out, there wouldn't be any sense in telling you any of this at all.

It was right after we finally got untangled from the Decoration Day parade and Daddy got Bodine back in the car and calmed down after he cavitated when he saw Miss Evie riding around in the Packard with the Negro in the purple suit. By now, you probably figured out it was Bo Manigualt, Dr. Indigo's boy, the same one who sassed Bodine down on Williman Island when he came to pick up those Savannah chickens. I hadn't figured it out just then, but I did after Bodine saw his chance to get even, which I'll get to after a bit.

Anyway, Daddy pulled up to the curb outside Elmore Alston's Sea Island Rexall Drug. Bodine right then being such damn poor company, I got out and followed Daddy inside.

There wasn't a God's soul in there 'cept Elmore and his new hired gal, Miss Marzette Goodwine. My, but she was a pretty thing, blue eyes and a handful of freckles thrown across her nose and hair like a new penny, and she was all round and sweet, not one of those hatchet-face redheads you always see. She was younger than Daddy, a couple of years too old to be my big sister, and even more from being my girlfriend, which is what I would have liked almost more than the way things finally turned out.

Anyway, we said our good mornin's and Daddy kind of looked the place over, like a good cop will do every time he walks into anyplace he hasn't been in awhile. He ran his eyes over Miss Marzette a couple of times, too, and don't think I was too young to notice.

Miss Marzette smelled like my momma, like peaches, or peach blossom honey, though that day I never got close enough to wind her. I caught Elmore Alston instead. Elmore Alston smelled like cough syrup. Daddy said Elmore would dip into the paregoric about quitting time, hold a spoonful over a kerosene lamp til he cooked the alcohol out of it and then eat the opium left over. We called him "Squinchy," from the way he kept his face drawed up in the morning.

"Marzette, Marzette, what's wrong with you, gal? You got time to lean, you got time to clean." Squinchy talked like a Negro, the way most of us did.

Miss Marzette was leaning on the counter, watching me and Daddy. I guess we would have turned a heart of stone. You know, the good looking young sheriff with no wife and a young tow-headed boy running barefoot. Those days I shucked my shoes each April, gimping along tender-footed at first, but by September running barefoot through the woods like an Indian. But she didn't have a heart of stone, no sir.

Daddy said something about the store being empty and Squinchy said something like: "White people stay home and niggers parade. They got all they need on the street."

And Daddy said maybe he could help some and Squinchy wrung a nervous little smile out of himself like he was about to make a twenty dollar sale.

But then Daddy asked about sunglasses.

Squinchy drew a blank. Then he said, "Marzette, what's wrong with you? Put up that broom and wait on the sheriff!"

Well, from the minute Miss Marzette saw Daddy, she was waiting, if you know what I mean. I figured she might wait quite a spell, too. But maybe not, 'cause redheads don't have as much patience as most folks.

Anyway, Miss Marzette, all lit up orange like an October moonrise, slipped behind the counter and hauled out a box of sunglasses. There was a war that year and most of them were those aviator types, smoky gray and green and expensive.

But then Daddy said he wanted some blue ones and, just like Squinchy, Marzette drew a blank. But then she ducked down below the counter and came up with a pair, wire-rimmed and small, like those frames you see on pictures of Benjamin Franklin. She blew the dust off of them and slid them towards Daddy. He picked them up and put them on and flashed Miss Marzette his best grin. My, but he looked good.

"Why in the world," Miss Marzette said, "would you want to cover up those baby blues?"

Daddy touched the edge of his cap, kept grinning. He was looking at his reflection in the mirror behind the soda fountain.

"You know the last time I sold a pair of those?"

That got Daddy's attention. "When?" he said.

Miss Marzette's voice trailed off like she was Harley Davidson trying not to remember Cuffey Wiggins' name. "It's been awhile," she said.

Well, Daddy was stumped, temporarily, anyway. He paid for the glasses, two dollars and twenty-two cents, tipped his hat and maybe he winked at Miss Marzette, but none of us could see it behind that blue glass. And then we lit out for the river.

So there we were, fishing the wreck of the Lawrence. Daddy snagged a five-pound puppy drum, all silver and striped and full of fight. I caught three whiting, about two pounds each, about the best eating fish in the river, especially when Miss Althea rolls them in cornmeal and quick fries them in lard hot enough to smoke. Then Bodine tied into something real big.

There was one big snatch and the thing took off, slow and sure as a mule heading home. The line played out and the drag whined and Bodine started cussing and leaned into the rod, bent nearly double. After ten or fifteen minutes, Bodine got it stopped and then turned and began working it toward the boat. "It's one hell of a shark!" Bodine hollered, "Lil Mac, get the gaff!"

I dug it out from beneath the middle seat and passed it to Daddy.

I don't know what he wanted the gaff for. A shark will come

over the side thrashing and snapping and real soon there wouldn't be room in the boat for both him and us.

The thing made another run, straight down this time and glued itself to the bottom and you could've played a tune on the line. "Stingeree," Daddy said.

If you never seen a stingeree, then you never looked upon the face of Satan. Oozy and flop-gilled and mean-eyed with teeth that can crack a clam or take a finger clean off. They start out the size of a dinner plate and end up big as your kitchen table. They lay on the bottom and look like mud and if you step on one and he nails you, you'd a-wished you'd been snakebit instead. It hurts like hell and it won't heal and if you get blood poisoning, it'll kill you in a week. Old John Smith, the one who ran off with Pocahontas, stepped on one back in 1607. He had his men dig his grave and he lay in it for a week, and said, "Cover me up if I stop breathing."

Bodine put his back into the rod and broke the ray loose and it come up alongside the boat, big as a washtub, clacking his teeth and whipping that tail. Now you remember me saying how you can't worry and fish at the same time. But that don't mean you don't have to pay attention. Daddy was trying to get a gaff in the stingeree and Bodine was trying to get ahold of the hook with his pliers when the damn thing flopped over and before you could blink, it popped Bodine right in the back of the hand. His right hand, his gun hand, his billy stick hand, bad news for him, good news for upwards of a thousand Negroes.

Bodine howled and cussed and fell back into the boat and

the blood flew and the rod and the gaff and the stingeree went right for the bottom. Daddy leapt across the seat and grabbed Bodine and set him down hard.

It wasn't as bad as it might have been. The barb hit him right between the bones of his second and third finger but it did not break off like they most always do. But when it came out it stripped back the flesh and left a hole the size of dime full of some pretty nasty stuff. Bodine shook and sweated and ground his teeth while Daddy dosed him with a shot of Clorox, which hurts like hell, too, but neutralizes the poison.

Well, we were short a rig and short a gaff and one man had a hole in his hand. It was more or less typical of a Little Glory river trip, where you'd better factor in gators and sharks, sun and windburn, swamping, shoaling and marooning. It was beautiful, all right, but it was meaner than hell and over the years a whole lot of folks have gone down to that water and never come back. I could name you a dozen, the empty boats with one hip boot and the motor out of gas but still in gear; the boats turned upside down and blowed ashore; boats that simply disappeared and the bodies on the beach with noses and eyes all et up by the crabs from here to Ossabaw Island. But we were still alive and we had supper for all of us, Miss Althea and Harley Davidson, too, so Daddy hauled in the anchor and set Bodine in the middle seat and got the Elgin going.

We were running with the tide, now, and fairly flew along, moving about as fast as a boat would move back in 1942. We were about halfway to Albemarle, passing that broad creek up behind Bull Island when Daddy swung the tiller hard to starboard. I looked to read his face and he shot me a quick grin and asked how I was doing.

"Just fine, sir," I said, "but I'm getting a little peckish."

He nodded toward the bag of sandwiches beneath the seat, the bottom all soggy with bilgewater. Then he turned to Bodine. "How's that hand, Jim?"

Bodine held it up. It was wound up in a greasy rag and looked like a cannon swabber. "I ain't ready to cut it off yet, Mac."

"Well, if you all can just hang on an hour more, I got a little something I want to check on."

That's the way Daddy was. It's a God's wonder he ever got anything done. There was always just one more little thing—stopping by the office and getting ambushed by Rauls and the Reverend Billy Kinkaid, getting tangled up in the Decoration Day parade, then stopping by Squinchy's and getting ambushed by Miss Marzette. Each one more little thing generally turned out to be one hell of a big thing, and this time was no exception.

I fetched out the bag, and the sandwiches Miss Althea made had gone clean to hell, soppy white bread and stinky bologna you wouldn't feed your dog. But there was an apple in there and I ate it. It was a little salty, but cool and good. Daddy ran a mile or so up into Bull Creek, then cut the motor and put us up on a shell rake where he fed the Elgin another two gallons of fuel, then cranked her again and headed on up the river. We ran til the channel petered out into a confusion of little sidecreeks where the tide stopped and the bottom silted. He cut the motor again, grabbed an oar and poled us through an acre of rattling spartina, then out into the headwaters of the Mungin River on the other side. The tide had rose to brimming flood and now was sliding off in the earliest ebb and we rode the seabound water down toward Williman Island.

Then Daddy put us up into a twisty little tidal gut, winding way off toward the southwest. One turn, two, three, and then we found it. A little footbridge out in the highmarsh, boards and planks supported by the damnest collection of net floats, old life jackets and gallon glass jugs. If you got on it during flood tide, somebody a mile away would swear to Jesus you were walking on the water. Daddy cut the motor and stood up on the stern seat and Bodine stood up on his seat, too, and cussed one of his famous cusses. They stood looking at the footbridge for a long time and then Daddy said, "Indigo, you phony old bastard."

We were halfway up the Little Glory River, nearly home, when we met the great bouquets of Decoration Day flowers, floating along with the tide.

Chapter Seven

It was damn near dark by the time we got back to the landing. The sun had slid off toward Savannah, slipping behind a line of distant thunderheads, building great purple peaks and lavender canyons of air. Ten thousand acres of salt marsh stretched out below it all, green and glorious and almost endless, and way off to the west the little creeks caught the sky and glowed like shining slivers of cold rolled steel.

Daddy stood knee deep in the river, holding the bateau against the sucking ebbtide while Bodine labored over the winch with his one good hand. Clickety, clickety, click, the sodden hull rose from the water up onto the creaking trailer and the light failed and the first pinprick stars shimmered in the darkening east, way out over Grenadier Shoals.

Daddy lashed the bateau to the trailer and I climbed into the back seat and we rode west down the winding sand roads toward Albemarle. The ruts and swales and little mud wallers set the car to rocking like a boat in ocean swells and before too long I was way out on the deep blue water of dreams.

I was back on Grenadier Shoals and the tide was high

enough for the rollers to clear the banks and the waves were frothing white and green, busting against what was once the *Lawrence*. I was waiting for a strike and I looked up and there was Jesus coming to me across the water. He looked just like he did on those cards I got from my great aunt Gladys every Easter, all long-haired and sad-eyed and tan as any shrimper and the water swirled at his feet like he was skating along on a pair of porpoises. Then He smiled at me and waved like He was going to show me His best fishing drop. I looked for Daddy and Bodine and Bodine was not there. Then Daddy smiled and nodded like he was saying "Go ahead, son, go fishing with Jesus." And I stood up and reeled in and was about ready to step over the side of the boat when Jesus looked at me and said, "Yawp, scranch, and gawnk" and it was the police radio and not Jesus, at all.

I had been sleeping ten minutes, maybe fifteen, and man, if I was going to dream like that all the time, I'd lay down and sleep forever. But then there was that damn radio. Even if I was awake, I don't know if I could tell you what it said. Harley Davidson, down at the Albemarle docks one time watching a Spanish tuna boat unload, listened to the babble on the deck and turned to me and said, "I don't know what nation they is, Mr. Lil Mac, but they can spit out that Portygee most good as a Jew."

That's the way police radios sound to me. I reckon that's why they throw in so many numbers. What's your 20? And we got a 2750, or a 4450, or some other number that could mean anything from a broke down car to a filling station holdup.

So like I said, I didn't know what the hell it meant, but Bodine said "State Police" and Daddy stepped on the gas. Just like that time I was drifting off and Daddy told me about seeing Dr. Indigo walking on the water, I was up and hanging on the back of his seat like a spaniel.

Our red flashing cop light lit up the countryside we passed, like Sherman's torches must have done, though it would be a long, long time before I could see I was riding with the enemy that night. Daddy was the duly elected sheriff of Calhoun County and I was his son and Bodine was his deputy. Things were getting damn strange, but they was Negroes and we were buckra and we were the law.

Daddy kept the pedal down. Whoosh, the circling light went across the live oaks. Whop, it bounced off Blocker's storefront, where they advanced the Negroes credit at fifteen percent against cotton and tomatoes and watermelons and collard greens. Zip-zip, across the shanties along the road, doorframes and porch posts painted blue to keep back the spirits. Swish, across three dozen wild sets of eyes along the road, all primed for some private Decoration Day celebration.

Daddy let off the gas, briefly hit the brake and hung a sharp left on Seaside Road. His foot went down again and tires broke loose and the car shimmied like a fat gal does when she goes out to dance. And then Bodine said, "The Swing Low Sweet Juke Joint? Damn, Mac, that's a mean place."

Juke is African for dance, or maybe sing, I forget which. That's where we get jukebox and juke joint. White folks don't mind driving six or eight miles to their own joints, but back when I was a boy, very few Negroes had cars. Of course you'd see a few preachers or undertakers with big blue Buicks and now and then a zoot-suiter like Bo Manigualt with a Packard or a Caddy, but most of them walked or climbed onto the backs of field trucks, or hooked rides with white people.

So most every neighborhood had a juke joint. There were dozens of them scattered across the islands, with names like Soul Palace, The House of Joy, Saturday Night Confusion, and Humble Buck's Community Center Joint.

In those days we did not have likker by the drink, or at least legal likker by the drink, anywhere in South Carolina. White people had their private clubs, where you could join at the door for fifty cents and drink all night for a quarter a shot. A dozen years later I was up in Charleston in the Carolina Yacht Club, hooked over a glass of sour mash when two men in blue suits and red ties walked in the door carrying attaché cases. They sat at the bar and ordered a round. Then the bartender gave them each an unopened bottle and they stuck them in their cases, wrote him a receipt and left. Later on, I asked the bartender what the hell that was all about and he looked at me the way Harley Davidson did when I asked why he couldn't swim and said, "Why, son, that's a raid."

But the Negroes? You could see them at likker stores at closing time loading cases and cases of half pints into the backs of their wheezy pickups to sell at juke joints that were supposed to serve only beer and wine. Those likker stores were something else, too. The Baptists had the whole state buffaloed and you couldn't sell whiskey after dark and you couldn't put up a sign that said Whiskey for Sale. The stores opened at legal sunrise and shut down at legal sunset, just like the hours for shooting ducks, a different time every day. They had a big red ball outside and folks from somewhere else had a hell of a time figuring out where to get themselves a jug. We locals called them Sundown Stores and reckoned the red ball was the setting sun.

And then there was the moonshine, at about half price since there was no taxes on it, slippery looking white whiskey strong enough to get you to town if you ran out of gas. Every Negro had a patch of corn and every stalk had a spigot on it, Daddy said, which was only a slight exaggeration. "It ain't like you sto' bought likker," Miss Althea's man Willie Simmons told me once, "it don't make you all slobbery drunk."

Well, maybe not, but bad moonshine would drive you blind or kill you outright and if you got a juke joint full of Negroes full of shine, good or bad, somebody would likely get his back up over money or women or dope and haul out a straight razor or a knife and start cutting three ways, high, wide, and frequent. I remember sitting in Daddy's office one day when a Negro busted in a-hollering about a stabbing in some beer joint and Daddy knew soon enough there would be a revenge cutting, so he said, "Take him to the ice house and call me when there's two." And pretty soon the Negro comes back a-grinning and said, "You can come now, Capum." And Daddy did.

And another time when a giant of an oysterpicker, who could snap store-bought oars as fast as you could hand them to him, got likkered up and went after somebody and the other man ran off and hid on an oyster barge. Later that evening, the picker followed him and grabbed him by the hair and held him over the side so the blood wouldn't get all over the deck and cut his throat ear to ear.

Daddy tracked him down and arrested him and threw him in jail and the picker got religion and wanted to be baptized before they hung him. He was some shade of Baptist like most of the Negroes and only total immersion would do. Daddy figured he might try and run if they took him down to the river, so he slid the county boat off the trailer and filled it with water in the jailhouse yard. The preacher came and the elders came and a few of the bretheren and sisteren, too, but when the man went to step into the boat he slipped and fell with a mighty splash and the preacher started hollering "Gawd baptize um!"

Baptized or not, they led him out to the gallows on the appointed day. But when they sprung the trap the rope broke and the picker lay thrashing and gurgling beneath the scaffold. The preacher took this as another sign and that God not only baptized him, but He saved him, too. But Daddy got out the sentence and read it to the crowd and it said "hanged by the neck until dead." Since he obviously was still alive, the sentence had not been carried out yet. So, Daddy sent Bodine down to Billy Rhett's hardware for a stouter rope while everybody else stood around and watched him kick and gasp and claw at the noose. When Bodine got back, five or six men hauled the picker back onto the platform and they hung him again. But this time the rope was too thick to snap his neck and he hung there until he strangled. It was one hell of a thing and I'm damn glad I wasn't there to see it. I got enough nightmares as it is.

But here I am, way off track again.

The Swing Low Sweet Juke Joint was at the end of a long sandy track, way down past that little plank bridge where Seaside Road crosses Fish Haul Creek. It was typical of most, a slantindicular tin-roof building with Nehi Cola, Black Label Beer, and Bull of the Woods Chewing Tobacco signs tacked here and there, more to cover holes in the clapboards than for any advertising value. A half mile away Daddy cut the cop light, then the headlights, and finally the engine and we coasted into the yard.

Man, the place was a rocking. Willie Simmons used to spend Saturday nights at Jumpin' Jimmie's, another joint not too far from Little Glory. Finally, Daddy had enough of him all tore up and worthless on Sundays and he got after him about it. "Willie, what in the hell's the matter with you stumbling around drunk every Sunday morning?" And Willie looked at him with one bloodshot eye and said, "Well suh, Mr. Mac, if you could be a nigger for one Saturday night, you'd never want to be a white man again."

And sitting there in the squad car in the dark, listening to the raucous old blues on the jukebox and the whooping and laughing and hollering, catching a bit of fried mullet on the breeze, I was ready to believe it.

But damnit, Daddy was the law and he had a job to do. He turned to Bodine. "Jim, you set here with Lil Mac. I'll be right back."

"Wait a minute," Bodine said. "The State Police will be here directly."

"Long about daybreak," Daddy said.

"Too risky," Bodine said, "they getting tribal in there."

"Come daylight he'll be mighty scarce. I got to take him now." Then Daddy turned to me. "Want to help me out, bub?"

My heart did a double back flip. "Yessir!"

"Take off your hat."

I whipped it off my head.

"Now hold it over the dome light. I don't want nobody to see me open this door."

I slapped my cap over the light and cupped it with my hands while the butterflies played tag in my stomach.

Daddy eased open the door, stepped out and eased it shut once again. I put my hat back on my head.

"I don't like this, Mac," Bodine said. "Not one damn bit."

"I'll be fine," Daddy said. "Pass me my gun."

Bodine reached under the seat and came up with Daddy's gun rig, a basket weave belt and holster with a nickle-plated Colt .38. He didn't wear it much, but I'd seen him bust poker chips at thirty paces. Then he reached into his shirt pocket and pulled out those blue sunglasses.

"You lost your mind, Mac?" Bodine whispered. "You can't shoot in the dark with those!"

But Daddy was gone, buckling his gun rig as he slipped away in the dark, moving through the night like an Indian.

Lord God, what a man. I wondered if I would ever see him again.

The music stopped and the lights went out the instant Daddy cleared the doorsill. And then there was a flash in the windows and the dull thump of a gunshot. Then another. And another. And another.

I screamed til I thought I'd turn inside out.

Bodine held his head in his hands and rocked back and forth on the seat. "He's dead, oh, goddamnit, he's dead." He said it over and over.

Now don't you ever let anybody tell you the Age of Miracles has passed, 'cause I seen one that night. I was an orphan for ten seconds, then the lights came back on and Daddy came out the front door dragging a skinny Negro by the scruff of the neck.

"Shot at the sheriff?" Bodine hollered. "What the hell got into him?"

Daddy grinned and his blue glasses caught the moonlight. "Oh, I reckon he's been to New York."

Chapter Eight

Well, that's how Daddy got to be bulletproof. Or at least, that's what the Negroes said. From the Little Glory River to the Georgia line the story was the same. Four shots at point blank range and the bullets just bounced off his chest. Ok, you'd say it was just plain dumb luck. Daddy wore his blue glasses and the man thought Daddy had the power and got shakey and missed. But the facts speak for themselves. Four shots fired and not a hair cut. Daddy never even drew his gun that night and nobody ever shot at him again.

The man that did it? Hell, I can't even remember his name. They said he was born around here but got Philly Fever and went to New York and stuck up a pawnshop and stole a car to get back home. The judge sent him up for armed robbery, but Daddy wouldn't let the solicitor add attempted murder to the charges. Daddy stood up in court and said it was just like he had got shot at from ten miles away. The man had no chance of hitting him, so there was no murder attempted. That helped the story along some, too.

Daddy got real fond of those blue glasses, as you might

imagine. In time he would use them just like Dr. Indigo did that day in court, but for making people talk rather than seize up. I seen the day when he could walk into a room, put on those glasses and a murderer would weep and blubber and the stenographer couldn't get it down fast enough.

But I'm getting a little ahead of myself. Right after Daddy found that footbridge out in the highmarsh, he went after Dr. Indigo. He lay in the weeds outside Indigo's house on Hsupah Plantation one afternoon and watched the comings and goings. The ticks were bad and the chiggers were worse and the deer flies gave him absolute hell. He stood it for an hour, or so, before the bugs ran him and he learned just enough to want to learn more. There was quite a crowd, he said, cars with Georgia and Virginia and Tennessee and even New York license plates and a stream of Negroes beating a path to the door.

Daddy had a deal with a cabbie named Samuel Dibble. Segregation was in pungent full flower those days. If a man had a service station, he had to have four bathrooms: White men, white women, black men, black women. A doctor or a lawyer had two waiting rooms and four bathrooms. And every place always had two water fountains and the ones marked "Colored" generally gave lukewarm water while the ones for whites ran cold. And of course, there were two school systems even if all the kids got together after school like me and Harley did. This all cost a lot of money, and it beats the hell out of me why white southerners, poor since General Sherman, would go to such expense, we and the Negroes being so damn near the same and all.

But I guess that don't really matter. I'll tell it to you straight up, not the way I'd a had it, if I made up the rules. Rauls had two sets of drivers and tried to figure out which to send out from the voices and addresses he got over the phone. Mix-ups were inevitable. If somebody said Smalls, you'd know his grand-daddy took the name of Robert Smalls, who stole that Confederate gunboat and turned it over to the Yankees. Lesesne and Huguenin and Desaussure had come down from French Protestants and were about as white as you can get. But then there were Greens, kin to Silas Green from New Orleans, the Negro minstrel singer; and there were Greenes, kin to the Revolutionary War general. Pinckneys, of course, were hopeless. They were good masters with lots of slaves and the slaves took their last name when General Sherman said they must have one. The white Pinckneys were about like the Heywards, mar-rying their cousins 'cause they were the only ones good enough for them. They got run down and thinned out and their former slaves had about a dozen children apiece and now you can't hardly find a white Pinckney in the Charleston phone book.

This Samuel Dibble was a Negro, of course. He hauled other Negroes around Ward Six, and sometimes out onto the islands. Whenever Sam saw or heard anything that might be even remotely interesting, he'd give report and hit Daddy up for a little likker money, which Rauls would get, if Rauls was sell-ing whiskey, which I believe he was. Of course Sam cooked all sorts of inflammatory nonsense, specially on Fridays when he was getting a little thirsty.

I was in the office one hot Friday afternoon, sometime in early June, 1942, when Sam Dibble busted in the door. "I seen it! I seen it!" he hollered.

Daddy was deep into paperwork, something he hated but always had to do. "Seen what, Sam?"

Sam licked his lips. "I seen me a German sub-mo-reen!"

Daddy put down his pencil. "Whoa, Sam. What you say?"

Sam nodded, sincerity fairly dripping off him. "A gen-you-wine German sub-mo-reen. I seen it, Mr. Mac, big as a battle-ship, wif men a-swarmin' like ants. I was pullin' crab pot and she blew like a porpoise and come pun-top the water right in the mouf of the Little Glory ribbuh!" He paused to let this sink in, and then said, "You got ten dollar?"

"Ten dollars? Damnit, Sam, I told you I'd give you five for keeping an eye on old Indigo!"

Sam got all twiss-mouf. "I kep' an eye on him, Mr. Mac. I swear I tried."

Daddy looked at the papers again, then slid them into a pile at the corner of his desk and leaned back in his chair.

"Well?"

"Mr. Mac, they used to come back to the cab blabberin' how great the doctor be, how he bring gal and money and luck. Now they ain't crack they teeth."

"How come? You tell him anything?"

"Nossir, boss, I ain' say nuthin'. He know you on to him."

"Well, how he know that?"

Sam thought a quarter minute. "He got The Sight, jus' like you."

Now, this was getting good. First Daddy was bulletproof, now he had The Sight. If you were born "wif de caul," as the

Negroes say, with the amniotic sack over your eyes, you had The Sight and you could tell the future and see ghosts. A man born with the caul will see spirits a dripping off tombstones and hanging from the live oak branches until they get to be as natural as a man with britches. You'll know all about the jack-mulater and the plateye and the hag, who slips her skin and rides you in your sleep and smothers you with her private parts night after night til you get so poor you can't hardly live.

Well, I don't have The Sight and I'm damn glad I don't. I got the past and I got the present and that's about all I can stand. And I got enough trouble with live people, never mind the dead ones. And Daddy? Well, I don't know how he was born, but now the Negroes thought he had The Sight and that was good enough.

Daddy nodded. "Well, you tell him I got The Sight, too, and he's got trouble coming."

Samuel Dibble looked about the way Jonathan Polite did when he saw Dr. Indigo in court. "Oh Lordy, Mr. Mac! You want me to tell him that?"

Daddy looked Sam square in the eye. "Yep," he said.

There was a long pause, then Sam's head bobbed like a fishing float when a slab bream nibbles. "Yessir, Mr. Mac, I shore will." Then he paused again and swallowed hard. "I'll tell him soon as he axe."

"Well, if he got The Sight, he won't have to ask and you won't have to say. Meanwhile you count cars and people and remember dates and times. Write it all down."

Sam drew a blank, so Daddy said, "You can read and write,

can't you?"

Sam's face brightened. "Yassuh, I shore can."

Daddy pointed through the window to the front to the squad car, parked close to the building. "What that say?"

Sam stooped, squinted, and rocked back and forth and read the grill like it was an eye chart. "D-O-D-G-E."

"What's that say?"

"Che-bo-let," Sam gravely pronounced. "You got my ten dollar?"

"Sam, I done give you five dollars for watching Indigo."

"But I seen me a German sub-mo-rine!"

Samuel Dibble went away shaking his head and mumbling to himself, cussing the buckra, probably, from Julius Caesar all the way down to Adolph Hitler. He was halfway down the hall when I heard him suddenly shift gears, yassuh, good afternoon suh and how's that hand doing and all that. It was Bodine on his way back from the Post Office. Bodine might have had his right hand all up in bandages, but he would likely get them off someday and nobody wanted to take any chances.

Bodine came into the office, grumbling like a bull gator too late in the breeding season to get himself any. Daddy was back whittling on the paperwork. "How's that hand doing?"

Judging from the past ninety seconds, it might have been the hundredth time he got asked that in the last eight hours. "Goddamnit, Mac, I used to be a good man in a tight spot. Now all I do is run errands." Bodine held up his hand. There was a four inch square of gauze across his knuckles with a sickly yellow green puss the size of a quarter weeping through the middle. His fingers were swollen til his knuckles looked like dimples.

Daddy sucked his teeth and shook his head. "What we get in the mail?"

Bodine used his one good hand, his teeth, and a couple of fingers of his bad one to sort through the pile. "A bill for gas from Lonnie Mulligan, the *Palmetto Post*, the *Hound Dog Report*...."

The *Hound Dog* was a publication from the State Police, a list of who was running from who and why. There were pictures when they could get them, mostly Negroes, all shiney and fierce, wanted for robbing and raping and raising hell. White folks seemed to be able to stay out of it, not 'cause they were any less criminal, of course, but for hiring lawyers and cutting deals. Now we call it plea-bargaining, but back then it was just what you got from being white. Anyway, Daddy fanned through it without seeing anybody he knew.

Then Bodine laid the *Palmetto Post* upon his desk and thumped the headline with his good hand, twenty-four point type of some of old Will Mahoney's best: "Devil Krauts Sink Tanker off Jacksonville."

There might have been two Denmarks and two Norways, but there was only one Jacksonville, about a day's drive down US 17. Daddy fanned through the article and read a paragraph here and there. The *Eli Whitney* was running dark, but the Krauts must have spotted her against the lights of Jacksonville Beach. There was no warning, just a flash of fire and ten men dead, another dozen picked up by the Coast Guard, an oil slick from St. Mary's to Fernandina and the lights were going out all up and down the coast.

"Damn," Bodine said. "A general blackout. Mac, this is getting close."

Suddenly, a bootlegger and a voodoo doctor did not seem so important any more. But we weren't done with Old Indigo yet, not by a damn sight. Next in the pile of mail was the report from the state lab on that little packet Indigo had slipped Daddy at the trial.

Bodine tore it open and squinted at the paper. "Oh Sweet Suffering Christ!"

Daddy looked up from the *Palmetto Post*. "What's it say, Jim?"

Bodine's lips formed the words. He cussed again. "It's dirt."

"Dirt?"

Bodine worked his way down the page. "Yep, Mac, dirt. And some kind of rep-tile skins." He drew the word out like he wasn't used to saying it. Daddy got this bumfuddled look. "Lizzard skins? Snakes?" He asked. "What else?"

"What you mean what else? Ain't that enough?"

"Well, no," Daddy said. "it ain't illegal."

"Hell, I thought it was dope!"

"I told you it weren't dope."

"Yeah, Mac, you sure did. But you didn't figure it was snake skins and dirt either." Bodine went back to the page. "Or crow feathers or gunpowder or match heads and some stuff they can't even figure out. Mac, what in the hell is going on?"

Well, I knew something was up and Daddy did too. He

walked to the phone. "Irma," he said, "Give me Sea Island Cab." And then when he got Rauls on the line, he said. "Rauls, we got us a Negro over at the jail that needs transport. Could you send somebody over?" That somebody was Samuel Dibble, Albemarle's only Negro cabbie.

Chapter Nine

It's damn funny how things work. Daddy wanted to know about Dr. Indigo and Samuel Dibble wanted to talk about a submarine. Then Daddy wanted to know about a submarine and Sam Dibble wanted to talk about Dr. Indigo. About an hour later, he came busting through the door hollering. "I seen a white woman in there!"

Normally, this was nothing short of astounding, seeing how a quality white woman didn't even go into a sundown store and buy her own gin. A man would have to do it and if she didn't have a relation, she would have to hire one of Rauls' white cabbies. OK, Sam might have seen some real high-yaller gal come down from New York or Philly or maybe New Orleans, or even some Yankee white woman who figured Dr. Indigo could get her husband back. Seeing how Daddy was so fixated on running up Dr. Indigo, you'd have thought he'd asked Sam Dibble the details. But Daddy had shifted gears. If there was a submarine out there somewhere, he wanted to know all about it.

Sam Dibble pretty much went over what he said the first time. He couldn't read and he damn sure couldn't swim, but he was drawn to the water like all of us down here. We grow up on it and we eat the fish and oysters and shrimp that come out of it and pretty soon our blood moves like the sea. Men get to roamin' and women get to lovin' and the Negroes get to cutting each other when the moon gets round and the nightbirds cry and tide creeps up through the highmarsh right into people's front yards.

You can break a man of loving that water if you put him on a shrimpboat or a pile driver or an oyster bateau and work him sixteen hours a day for twenty years. Maybe then he'll sit under a oak and drink Black Label and watch the river flow. But if there ain't no gale or rain or a hurricane, every chance we get, all of the rest of us head for the river.

Sam Dibble was no different. He might have worked for Rauls, but he ran trotlines for drumfish in the spring and crabbed every summer and in between he worked the sidecreeks with a net and sold mullet and shrimp and croaker out of the trunk of Rauls' cab to Negroes along a route from Albemarle to Tullifinny.

You put in your time out there on the big water and you will see some things. I seen manta rays as big as your garage door, leopard rays all spotted and wonderful and strange, hammerheads, tigers, makos, and jelly-fish and whales, waterspouts whipping from the low-hanging scud like long greasy ropes, and lightning so close you can hear it hiss when it hits the water. Sam Dibble was out in the mouth of the Little Glory, an hour or two after dawn, when the bubbles rose and the water bulged, and a Kraut U-boat, fully three hundred feet long, broke to the surface three quarters of a mile away.

That's what Sam Dibble said, anyway. Daddy might not have believed it the first time, but now he wasn't so sure. There's eighty foot of water there at low tide and the channel is wide enough for the Titanic to steam in circles.

"You see any numbers, Sam?"

"Yassuh, I seen numbers."

"What numbers?"

Sam scratched his head and looked off into middle distance. "Oh, I reckon either three or seventeen."

Daddy gave him ten bucks and walked to the phone. "Irma, give me the commander of the Fifth Naval District."

I was telling you how big things come to nothing and piddling-ass little things end up mule-kicking you into next Sunday. We had us a civil war and we all got burnt out and the Negroes set free. Eighty years later, we and the Negroes was working the same ground, the whites still bossing the Negroes and the Negroes real good at not being bossed. But a single foot sticking out of a pile of palmettoes, a wild Negro picking up a crate of chickens, and a pair of blue glasses changed everything. Of course I didn't know it then, but the minute Daddy picked up that phone, another little thing started cooking. There was just no end to it.

It took Irma quite a spell to find the number of the office up in the Charleston Navy Yard. Then Daddy had to go through a long string of other folks—ensigns, lieutenants, and captains—telling each one who he was and what he wanted and who he needed to talk to. Finally, he got the admiral on the phone. The admiral listened and sent him back to the ensign, the first man Daddy talked to. Samuel Dibble's submarine got entered as a "reported sighting," common as catfish that week the Whitney went down. After Sputnik, everybody saw flying saucers. Then it was Elvis. That year, you'd think the entire German U-boat fleet was just offshore.

And there were stories. Secret agents coming ashore in rubber boats, spies along the waterfront that radioed the submarines whenever a ship got underway, and the best of the bunch, the dead German sailor who washed ashore on Pawley's Island with ticket stubs in his pocket from a Charleston movie house. There was a German family dairy farming there, whose name I can't remember like Harley Davidson can't remember, who they thought might be slipping the Germans groceries. It went on and on. Folks got mighty jittery and kept an eye on the creek and their shotguns loaded. A government man came and shut down all the streetlights in Albemarle, and made you turn off your porch lights and shutter your windows that faced the river.

Finally, when we got news of a burning molasses tanker off Key West, I got a touch of sub-fever myself. Harley Davidson come to me one afternoon in a fine sweat. He said he spotted two of them up in the end of Horse Hole Creek. "Yessir, Mr. Lil Mac, they laying side by side like two pigs in a hawg yard. All black and greasy."

I reported to Daddy and asked if he wanted to call the admiral in Charleston. Daddy cocked his head the way a deer hound does when he sees you with a gun. "Where'd you say?"

"Way up in Hoss Hole Creek."

Daddy grinned. "Why, what's wrong with you bub? You can't get no German submarines way up in Hoss Hole Creek!"

"Maybe they midget submarines," I said. This time he laughed and turned and was about to walk away so then I shouted. "Why would Harley Davidson lie to me?"

Daddy stopped, turned and gave me one of those whup-ass looks, if you know what I mean. "Look here, boy. Don't pester me so." I guess I couldn't blame him for getting short like that. He had a lot on his mind and he was trying to be a daddy when what I needed was a momma, too. But then his face softened and he half smiled the way he did. "OK, Mr. Samuel Dibble Malcolm Edward McCloud the VII, I will give you money for a bottle. A bottle of Nehi, that is. You find me a German submarine in Hoss Hole Creek, and I'll pay up."

"How about Harley Davidson?"

"If he found two German submarines, I'll buy him a case."

They named Horse Hole Creek for the deep tidal pool that was up against the bluff on Secinger's Point where somebody's horse fell in and drowned years before. Horse Hole was a good two miles down the riverbank, all snakey and skeetery there where the red cedars and the mournful oaks hang out over the salt marsh, but the mud wasn't too deep and there weren't many shells; you couldn't get lost like you might if you lit out through the woods. We had three hours of daylight left, so I got my pellet rifle and my knife and a canteen full of water and Harley Davidson got a hatchet and a forked stick for the moccasins and we headed north along the bank of the Little Glory River.

"You see any Germans hanging around?" I asked.

Harley was beating the snakes out of a saw palmetto thicket, making a racket like he was wading through a pile of Venetian blinds. "No sir, Mr. Lil Mac, I ain't seen a one of them. But they got to be here somewheres. What you reckon they look like?

"'Bout like us, I reckon."

"No," he said. "You reckon?"

"Sure. I seen 'em in the *Post*. Just like us, 'cept they blonde and ornery."

"Oh Lordy, Mr. Lil Mac. That pellet popper do us any good?"

"It'll sting the shit out of 'em." I was back to cussing, again. "Tell me 'bout those damn submarines. What they look like?"

"They iron and all put together with rivets. They got seats in 'em and damn big rudders on the back end." Harley stooped and read the mud. "Ooohh, Mr. Lil Mac, looky here."

Little cloven hoof marks were pegged into the mud everywhere. "Deer," I said.

Harley shook his head. "No, Mr. Lil Mac, look at this."

There was a nose print in the soft mud, round and big as a donut, two little dimples right in the middle. Harley began looking for a tree to climb. "Hawgs, Mr. Lil Mac, them damn ol' wild hawgs."

Another twenty steps and there was pig sign everywhere—hoof marks, more nose prints and rooting, lordy, like somebody had gone through with a disc harrow, and the bark torn off trees where the boars had polished their tusks.

The Spanish had hogs penned up on the decks of their

galleons. When they got over here in the 1500s, they turned them loose so they could come back later for fresh pork. Pigs got loose from the colonial plantations and a Negro never ever fenced a hog. Then the Yankees came down after the war with Russian boars to liven up the bloodlines and, Lordy, they look more like a werewolf than a barnyard pig, your absolute equal in a ham chewing contest, so damn mean they root rattlesnakes out from under logs and put their foot on 'em and start eating and snakebites don't bother them at all.

"Come on Mr. Lil Mac," Harley said. "Let's get the hell out of here."

We did. Down the riverbank towards Horse Hole, Harley looking over his shoulder and jumping at every bird rustle in the bushes, me with my pellet rifle at high port, weather eye out for German sailors and wild pigs.

About a hundred yards from the hole, Harley and I cut back into the woods, then worked towards the river on our bellies. We crept to the edge and looked over the bluff. There below us were two iron Navy lifeboats, left over from the first war, I reckon, sunk and covered all over with pungo mud like black axle grease.

"What I tell you, Mr. Lil Mac, there they is."

I stood up. "Hell, Harley, they ain't no damn submarines!"

"They ain't?"

It was dark by the time we got back to Little Glory. Harley Davidson wandered off on home, but I had to go to Daddy and fess-up. I'd been a jackass, I didn't listen to him, and I'd have better sense next time. You know, all of that.

He was on the phone when I came slinking down the hall. "Daddy," I said.

He scowled and held up his hand like a cop stopping oncoming traffic and then I was doubly ashamed. I turned away and did battle with tears that almost got the best of me, even though I was too old to cry like that any more.

"Where'd you get him?" Daddy asked. Then he nodded out of habit like the man on the other end of the line could see him. "What you got him booked for?"

The phone squawked and popped. I couldn't make out the words or tell who it was. Daddy listened awhile then said, "Hell, turn him loose! Turn him loose right now!"

Daddy hung up the phone and walked to the kitchen and poured himself a good shot of brown likker. He cut it with a splash of water, took a long pull. I had snuck in behind him and was standing by the door. "Bodine's picked up Bo Manigualt," he said.

Chapter Ten

Bodine turned Bo Manigualt loose, but Bo Manigault never made it home. They found his car on the morning low tide, upside down, way out in the marsh where the road takes that swing to the east before it crosses the Tullifinny bridge. Bo was in the backseat, Daddy said, and he had clawed the headliner to ribbons, thinking somehow it was the door. And then he had just given up and curled up into a little ball and drowned.

It was entirely obvious: Bo Manigault was drunk and ran off the road. Yeah, I know, today they would be a coroner's inquest and a grand jury investigation, articles in the paper and either Daddy or Bodine would have lost their jobs, maybe both. But in those days it was just another dead Negro and everybody was so damn sorry for a couple of days.

Lonnie Mulligan backed his tow truck down the bank of the causeway and put on his shrimping boots and bogged out and got two hundred feet of cable onto the back bumper, and the Packard came out of the cordgrass sliding on its roof. The back glass was gone and the windshield was gone and the roof scooped up the pungo and the reeds and the roots, and by the time they got it up onto the road, Daddy had to run to Billy Rhett's hardware for shovels so they could get the body out. Then old Elias Sherman, the Negro undertaker down on the islands, came and got the body and there was some praying and some preaching and then they put him in the ground.

But not quite.

There were, of course, minor details. Somebody had beat the living hell out of Bo Manigault. Officially, it was from the brawl that got him arrested in the first place. Daddy picked up Sam Smalls, a brickmason with arms big as some peoples' legs, who might have broke Bo's nose in a tussle out at the Swing Low Sweet Juke Joint. But Daddy figured there was more to it. Maybe he had The Sight, after all. Daddy reckoned Bodine beat him, turned him loose, and then ran him off the road.

Of course, Daddy couldn't prove it and had he tried Bodine would have said, "Well hell, Mac, you said turn him loose and I turned him loose." Then Daddy's fanny would have been in the sling, since he had not asked if Bo was still too drunk to drive. But he didn't and now Dr. Indigo's only son was dead as a mullet. There was other stuff, too, stuff I still haven't figured out, yet. But I'll get to it after a while and tell it to you straight and you make sense out of it if you can.

Whatever passed between Daddy and Bodine, I never heard. But I can tell you there was an uneasy truce between them for a couple of days. Daddy got so itchy he started wearing his gun whenever he was in town. I don't know if he figured on using it on Bodine, or not, but as it turned out, he did not have to, 'cause Bodine went over to see Miss Evie and she took a shot at him with a nickel-plated .25 automatic at three in the morning.

It wasn't much of a gun, I reckon, like most of them Negro pistols in those days. Daddy had a bushel of them he took off of people over the years. They were under his desk at the office, the damdest bunch of clappusses you ever did see. Spanish copies of Colts old and loose as your grand-daddy's knees, rusty relics with wads of friction tape for grips, and chrome-plated Saturday Night Specials that might fire and might not—if you could find shells to fit them. Daddy finally got disgusted and took them up to Orangeburg and sold the whole mess to a pawnbroker for a hundred and twenty bucks, pretty good money in those days, with the check made out to the Calhoun County Treasurer, so nobody could give any duff about it.

Of course, Daddy peeled off a couple of the best pistols and stuck them in his top drawer, hoping someday he could make them shoot. He finally got one to work, after a fashion. The cylinder wouldn't line up with the barrel and it would peel away about half the bullet and send it off at right angles to the line of fire, so he gave up on it and threw it into the Little Glory River. I reckon it's still out there. Damned if I know what happened to the other one. Guns got a way of getting away from you, pistols especially.

The rest of them probably got sold again, and maybe some might have even ended up killing somebody. But they were out of Calhoun County, and that's what Daddy cared about. The county line was the Seaboard tracks at Yemassee and I asked Daddy once what would happen if a train killed a man right square in the middle of the ties. And he said the first sheriff on the scene would roll the body over into the other man's county and spare himself the paperwork. That's the way we did it back then.

Anyway, that bullet missed Bodine by a foot or two, even though he had no blue glasses. But two blocks away, Miss Roberta Simmons had a bull tethered to her back steps. Miss Roberta had grown up driving oxen over on the islands, and could cuss them along pretty good. Now that there was gas rationing, Miss Roberta had hopes of making the bull into an ox and breaking him to harness if the war lasted long enough.

But she never quite got around to it. The bull's bullhood hung way down into the fennel, a sight to behold, like a couple of baseballs in a long sock. Miss Evie's shot passed through the rear wall of her house—Bodine being, as he must have been, in the back corner of the bedroom—and crossing two vacant lots, struck the bull in his nether regions. The bull bellered and took off through the neighbor's clothes line, twenty feet of rope and assorted laundry trailing from his horns, the remains of half of Miss Roberta's back stoop in tow. A hen house and an outhouse were casualties before the bull got one of Miss Roberta's porch pickets tangled in the cemetery fence and there he stopped and bellered til Miss Roberta came and led him home.

About halfway down the front steps, with all the crashing and bellering in the background, Bodine decided there would be no charges pressed, but no sooner did he get back home than Miss Roberta called him and politely suggested someone might owe her compensation. Bodine had to come out and file a report in the morning and how the man did it with a straight face is beyond me. I saw what he wrote up in his childish script, and I have it here somewhere if I would take the time to find it. "A accidental shot fired by one Evie Washington, did stripe..." and that is crossed out and "strike" written "... the rear end of a bull owned by Miss Roberta Simmons." By god, he should have been president.

Of course, Bodine was able to weasel out, him not firing the shot, and all. The magistrate found against Miss Evie, and she rowed a bateau out into the Little Glory and went fishing and looked over the side and the pistol, great Gawd a-mighty, fell "clean ober-bode."

So Miss Evie had no more pistol and she had to come up with twelve dollars and seventy-five cents for the porch and the outhouse and the hen house. Maybe she'd have given Bodine more lovin' if he had paid the damages, but the shooting had him boogered and he stayed away. Damn if I blame him, no matter how good she might have been.

Well, Bodine kept himself out of Ward Six, and hardly a white man would even drive by Miss Evie's house, anymore. But never did a shooting do a woman so much good. There was a long line of Negroes wanting to get one up on Bodine, and for the next six weeks solid, the bucks beat a path to her door. You know, like they were saying, "He might of busted my haid but I done spote he woman." Soon enough though, a man going out cut a man coming in and the novelty wore thin. Daddy had to put her on a bus for Macon and it was pretty blue in Ward Six for awhile. I don't know what ever happened to her, but somebody swore they saw her in a Buick convertible with Pigmeat Markham, the lead singer for the Thirteen Screaming Niggers, a big hit in the white beach pavilions right after the war. But I'm getting ahead of myself again.

Anyway, Bodine sort a withered. He wasn't about to drop over, or nothing, but he got sulky and listless and wore out easy. I mean, he hardly amounted to nothing some days. But he pulled his duty like he always did. Hell, he had to, he was the only deputy. But I saw the little things, like Daddy getting the jail keys when Bodine was off duty, and setting him off on projects that weren't likely to 'mount to much. There was the mail, of course, and the fan belts for the squad car and the chicken necks and rice and white bread for the prisoner, whenever there was one, which was not often, and watching the draftees get on the bus to Fort Jackson at four thirty in the morning. There were more and more of them that year and some of the Negroes got pretty uppity and it helped to have the law around.

But like I said, things got back to normal pretty quick—for the white folks, anyway. I finally told Daddy about Harley Davidson's German submarines being nothing but old Navy lifeboats, but I eased the news and my great embarrassment with news about the wild hogs.

Now, a wild hog is a fine thing to have, dead anyway. The meat is dark and the fat all marbled in like it is on good beef. You can cook him outside on hickory coals and dose him up with honey mustard barbeque sauce. You can save the scraps and mix them with venison for sausage that would make Old Wade Hampton rise from his grave and smack his lips. You can slice him thin or you can slice him thick, but whichever way you eat him, once you hang your lip over a plate of wild hog, you'll never buy pork at the grocery store again. So, one evening after work, Daddy got the shotgun—a fine old L. C. Smith double twelve—loaded his pockets with buckshot, and walked down to Horse Hole and poked around in the woods. He never saw so much as a hair, but he knew another spot across the river and, a couple of days later, he took me along when he went after them.

I carried my pellet rifle, of course. I kept it with me those days, them Germans being so close, and all. A man came through town and held a meeting at the Breeze Theater and all us white boys went. This was total war, he said, and over in England, little boys were getting blown to bits by German bombs and they were freezing to death out in Russia and the least we could do was volunteer to help beat that damn Hitler and the flat-face Japs, a mad race of sub-humans, he called them, hell-bent on destroying the world.

Well, I got war fever again and signed up to be an Official Junior Air Raid Warden so I could have the thirty-two photos of military planes, the I-D chart, the altitude height finder, the flight direction indicator, the logbook, armband, and the metal sign that would make the porch on the Little Glory house an official observation post. But everybody wanted to do that and they made me an Official Junior Blackout Compliance Warden, instead.

Anytime I was in town after dark, which was not often, I was supposed to put on my armband and walk along the riverbank and if a light showed anywhere, I was to knock on the door and tell them how the *Eli Whitney* took that torpedo off Jacksonville beach when folks didn't turn their lights out. And then I was supposed to read from a little book they gave me, about how Loose Lips Sink Ships, and how to keep an eye out for suspicious persons and German submarines. Well, by then I'd had a belly full of German submarines and I don't know how I would have gotten up the gumption to tell anybody had I actually seen one. But as it turned out, I didn't get much of a chance to be an Official Junior Blackout Compliance Warden, which is the next part of the story.

We took the rickety old bridge across the Tullifinny where the skid marks from Bo Manigualt's Packard still lay in the road like long black stripes to hell and the furrows from his tires went way out into the pungo and the marsh was all flattened down where the car finally came to rest. I did not say nothing and Daddy didn't either and then we passed the First African Baptist and saw the hearse and the mourners knotted up around it and we knew it was the day they were burying him. Maybe Daddy should have gone to that funeral, but he didn't. We went pig hunting instead.

Daddy turned right at the church, then went a mile or two down the sandy ruts, his head out the window and one eye on the ground. The road dipped into this little swale, then crossed a culvert and he pulled over under a live oak where we'd have some shade. It was hotter than blazes, and if we got us a hog, it would have to be close to the road where we could gut it, wrestle it out, and get it back to the ice house before it soured on us.

It was a perfect spot for hogs on a summer day, the tupeloes and soft maple all thick and shady and the low ground spongy and wet where a hog could waller and cool off and plaster himself with mud so the skeeters couldn't get to him.

I say if *we* got us a hog, but it was going to be just Daddy, not the both of us. There weren't no way he was going to let me into those woods. "No, bub," he said, "I'd have to be watching after you and not myself. A man can't be too careful messing with them wild pigs."

"Aw, come on, Daddy!" I said. "I can pop 'em with my pellet gun."

"Yeah you can," he said, "but I ain't after squirrels. That old boar will eat you up and pick his teeth with your gun when he's done."

I stood on one foot, then the other, waved the gun around. "Daddy, you won't let him do that."

"No, I won't, but I might get gnawed on keeping him off you and I ain't up to getting gnawed on today." He grinned one of those half grins of his. "You get your scrawny butt into the truck and you stay there. I'll be back directly."

And so off he went, picking his way upwind, moving like an Injun, moving like he did that night outside the Swing Low Sweet Juke Joint. Sure, I was mad 'cause he wouldn't take me, but I was mighty proud of him, anyway, all beady-eyed, quiet, and serious, the gun at the ready, his thumb on the safety and a finger on the trigger. I figured he'd have us pork before too long.

I stood in the pickup box and held my gun the way he did.

I picked out a leaf and kept my eye on it and brought up the gun without looking at it and got the leaf in the sights and *pip* there was a hole in it, just like that. I pumped it up again, eight or nine times, the lever getting stiffer with each stroke. I opened the action and slipped in a pellet, shaped like an hourglass and big as a pencil eraser. That's when I heard the hog grunt.

"OK," Daddy said, "don't get out of the truck," but I did anyway. A hog can't see nothing, but he's got a nose like a hound and ears like radar. I figured one had heard Daddy coming and slipped around and winded him and was backtracking out of the woods. I knew I couldn't kill him with the pellet gun, but I could raise hell with him and send him back to Daddy and Daddy would kill it for sure.

I was a dozen yards from the tailgate when I realized it wasn't a very good idea. There wasn't one hog, but six or eight of them—a boar, a sow, and a long string of twenty pound pigs.

It was the damnedest thing I ever seen. They come through the woods at a pretty good clip, trotting little pig steps, each pig but the first with its nose pretty well stuck up the fanny of the pig in front of him. There was nothing much to do but shoot, so I set my sights in the middle of that boar's nose and pulled the trigger.

Now, I don't know if I really expected to turn the hog back to Daddy. But if I was looking for him to wheel and run, I was severely disappointed. He snorted and went straight up in the air and turned on the sow and such a commotion you never heard, them a squealing and thrashing and the little pigs all running around in circles and falling over each other and snapping at each other, too. I was thirty feet away and I could hear them teeth just a poppin'.

I don't know how long I stood there with my jaw hanging, but pretty soon I figured I might need another shot. I was about halfway through the second pump when they saw me.

Don't let nobody tell you a pig can't run. Here they come, a boiling like hornets, the boar in the lead, halfway to me before I could even get turned around. But once I got to moving, I moved, too, and it's a God's wonder my feet did me any good at all, them being such a short time on the ground.

I knew they were gaining, but I dasn't look back. Click, click, the pig teeth went and I jumped for the tailgate just as the boar made a hook at my left leg.

I reckon that's what he did, anyway. I'll just tell you what I remember. Sixty-odd years later, it's bad enough to still wake me up sometimes. I went headfirst into the truck and when I came to I was flopped the other way, flat on my back, head on the tailgate. I couldn't move and the boar was trying to eat my face. I did not know it just yet, but the inside of my left leg was cut from knee most to my nubbins. And I was about to bleed to death.

The hog got his front feet up beside my ears and lunged at my face and tried to jump up in the truck, but he could not quite make it. Snap, snap and I could see the yellow tusks out of the corner of my eyes and his breath smelled like he'd been eating dead fish down along the creek. I threw my arm across my eyes and he knicked it once and then the shotgun went off and I heard more squealing and then it was all black.

It was real peaceful for a minute, kinda like when you wade out into the low tide surf and close your eyes and float belly up on the rocking swells and you can't tell where you stop and the water starts. Then I felt hands on me and my leg was burning and Daddy said, "Hang on, bub, hang on."

And then there was another voice with Daddy's and some arguing and then I heard a Negro say, "That boy's hog-cut and he's fixing to die."

And then Daddy started cussing and I felt someone's hands upon my leg and the pain faded and I opened my eyes and there was Daddy and Dr. Indigo looking down at me.

And then Dr. Indigo turned to Daddy and said, "You took my son. I give you back yours."

Chapter Eleven

Daddy told me about it afterwards, how Dr. Indigo pressed my torn flesh together, how the blood welled up between his fingers and then stopped, just like that. And Praise God, I'm here to tell you it was a laying on of hands better than anything cooked up by the Reverend Billy Kinkaid.

OK, I don't want to lose you now. I just told you that a voodoo doctor grabbed ahold of me and saved my life when I was hog-cut and fixing to die. I know you're likely saying, "Damn, you're telling me a good story, but don't stretch her too far, Mr. Lil Mac."

Well, I ain't stretching it. It's the God's Truth, like I said from the beginning. Way down in New Orleans, twenty years later, I met a Cajun woman who said her grand-momma could do the same thing, said they hauled her every axe-cut and machinery-tangled Negro for miles. "Don't let that nigger bleed in my kitchen," she'd shriek, "drag him out on the porch!" They would and she would pray and grab ahold of him and staunch the blood. And then there was Old Rasputin healing the crown prince of Russia, but I suppose you know that story already. If you don't, you ought to look it up. You'd see this wasn't the only time something like that ever happened. And I'd hate you to think I was a damn liar.

Well, they cut the seat cover into long strips and bound up my leg and hauled me to town. It was a long time before Daddy got around to fixing that seat, me riding on the padding and then on the springs that year I was on crutches. Well, it was only eight months, but it sure seemed longer.

I had to give up being an Official Junior Blackout Compliance Warden, so I deputized Harley Davidson in my place. He had a little paper flag left over from Decoration Day and I tacked it to an oak and I hung off the crutches there in the shade and swore him in. Then, I gave him my armband and my little book to read to the head of offending households and we saluted and I sent him to his duty.

That made me feel pretty damn good, better as the years piled up. Now, I never met Ralph Abernathy or Martin Luther King, Jr. I never was a Freedom Rider or a lunch counter deseg-regator, nor did I sit in the back of a bus in Chattanooga, Tennessee, and get my ass whupped like a woman I was sweet on once did. But I swore in the first and probably only Negro Official Junior Blackout Compliance Warden in American history.

That ain't much, you say? Well, it wasn't, but like most ever-thing else I am telling you, it started out small and then got to be so big, you couldn't hardly stand it.

But that was all later. For the first two weeks, I was laid up with stitches and couldn't walk without busting them loose.

Then, I got on crutches and hobbled back and forth to the bathroom and then to the front porch where I could look out onto the Little Glory, but not much else. One day, when I was sitting there in the rocker with my armpits rubbed raw and my stitches itching to drive me crazy, Daddy rattled up the driveway and walked out onto the porch, all lit up and taking steps four feet long. He had made a social call on Dr. Indigo, he said. Of course, I was so damn pitiful, I weaseled the story out of him right away.

He drove right up the driveway, he said, right past the bushes where the bugs had give him hell not too long before. He walked right up and knocked on the door. There were other folks there, too, a yard full of them. It wasn't quite the Williman Island stampede, but they didn't waste no time in leaving.

Lord God Amighty, I wish I could have been there when they met face to face and didn't have a half dead boy to distract them. Daddy was bulletproof. Daddy had The Sight. Now the Negroes were saying Daddy killed Bo Manigault with the Blue Root.

Now that I told you that, I better tell you the rest of it. There was all kinds of ju-ju going around in those days, some good, some bad. There were standards like the Money Come to Me Root, the Follow Me Boy and another love charm called Essence of Bend Over. There was Steady Work, Law Stay Away, Peaceful Home, John the Conqueror, High John the Conqueror, and Devil Be Gone. Those were the good ones. Then there was the Shut Your Mouth Special like Dr. Indigo threw on Jonathan Polite, the Death Unto Mine Enemies, the Seven Needles Suffering Root, and Satan Come Unto Thine Own. That last one was nasty. It'd make you have sex with a she-devil while you slept and pretty soon you'd take to likker and dope and stick up a filling station and they'd be a-hanging or the 'lectric chair.

This was serious as handling a stingeree and you had to watch what you were doing or else it could bust loose and get you, too. About the time I finally graduated from high school, two men got into a fight in a Savannah juke joint and one man threw a Devil Come Unto Thine Own on another. Of course, the man who got rooted died, but the man who threw the root died, too. And then two brothers got shot while robbing a likker store and two more got drunk up and didn't stop when they crossed the Seaboard tracks and got killed by the East Coast Champion and that was six men dead.

The Blue Root was the very worst of the worst, reputed to make chickens stop laying and to make cows and wells go dry. If somebody threw the Blue Root on you, you were good as dead. Or, if you didn't drop over from a heart attack or a stroke, pretty soon your troubles would gang up on you and you'd take to your bed and stop eating and drinking and then you'd be good as gone.

Some of the roots you could throw by remote control, you know, work something up in private and root somebody clean across town. Some of them, like the Shut Your Mouth Special and the High Chewing John, you mouthed in the presence of your victim. But the Blue Root was too powerful for that. You'd have go out to the graveyard and get dirt from a criminal's grave just after midnight. You'd leave an offering so the spirit wouldn't follow you home and feed the dirt with Red Devil lye or sulphur or gunpowder or match heads and mix it with hair or fingernail clippings from the one you wanted to root and sew it all up in a blue flannel bag the size of a peach pit. Then you had to put it in their clothes or hide it in their car or bury it beneath their front steps so it would work on them every time they came and went. The Negroes whispered that Daddy slipped Bo Manigault the Blue Root and that's why he drownded himself out in the high tide pungo.

Well, you can imagine the fix the doctor was in. He had locked horns with Daddy and come up short a boy. Bo Manigault, as trifling as he was, would have maybe someday straightened up and received the power coming down the long generations all the way from Old John Domingo. The word had got around pretty good and there would be Negroes from Charleston to St. Augustine awaiting the results. Would the doctor root the whole county, from the judge to the Church of the Cross Sunday School Superintendent? Would he put some kind of special root on Daddy, make his head turn around backwards and have him walk down the street barking like a dog? Would he put the Seven Needles Suffering Root on me and make my hog-cut infect and me get blood poisoning and die? Well, you know he wouldn't have hardly killed me, since he saved my life in the first place, but maybe not everybody knew that.

So they waited and not a damn thing happened. Nothing

they could see, anyway. No fires, no murders, no sudden death. That was just fine with me. But soon enough, I figured it wasn't about Lil Mac. Sure, he paid me special interest. I got where I could make polite conversation and he would ask about my leg and nod and smile and all I could see was my reflection in his blue glasses. Maybe if I would have had the nerve to sass him a little, he'd a-swatted me on the back of the head just like Miss Althea did. But it was Daddy Dr. Indigo wanted. I was just a way of getting to him. I'm not complaining, you understand, just telling you the way it was.

But like I said, stuff was going on. Daddy went out there and sat a spell and came home and I was all cooped up and miserable, so he told me another one of his stories, talking of candles and powders and herbs and snakes in jars and a Rise Up and Walk root Dr. Indigo was making for Roosevelt.

But Indigo was stumped. He had to know what polio looked like and he had to get a lock of the president's hair. He asked Daddy if he could help out, being sheriff, and all.

I was out of the rocker in a flash, sliding for the bookshelf on my fanny. I pulled the P volume of the Britannica off the shelf and scooted back to the porch. Daddy flipped the pages and found it right there on page 401, a picture of the polio bacillus. It didn't look like much, just a bunch of fuzzy dots all strung together with some kind of slime. Daddy took it out to Dr. Indigo's, but he couldn't get the hair and Roosevelt never walked again. A year or two later, he keeled over and died down in Warm Springs, Georgia, not too far from here. That liked to broke Old Indigo's heart, but by then he had his own troubles, which I'll get to after a bit.

Well, Indigo might have saved my life, and he might have been working on Roosevelt, but Daddy was still a cop and always a little suspicious. So when it came to bringing me to meet Dr. Indigo, he wanted it to be on neutral ground. Besides, after that go round with the hogs, he damn sure wasn't going to have me gimping and stumbling around a kitchen with a bunch of jarred copperheads. So he had Miss Althea make us up a basket for the beach.

Miss Althea was stirring the second scoop of sugar into the tea. "Where you say you going, Mr. Mac?"

"Goin' to have us a feedin' on the ground." Daddy said. "You throw in another half a chicken and come along."

Miss Althea nosed the kettle. "I kin feed Pharaoh army with this big bird. Where you all goin?"

Daddy played her like a fish, like a fiddle. "Oh, we figured Capers Island."

Miss Althea snorted. "Way out there?" It was more condemnation than question.

I was half wild and sassy, finally getting out of the house. "That old ocean is mighty big, Miss Althea."

She took a swat at me with her chicken fork. "Go 'long with you, boy; I done seen 'em."

You know, I never hardly knew a Negro who enjoyed the beach. The heat doesn't get to them and they don't sunburn, but they can't swim and they're scared of sharks and Africa is just beyond the next sunrise. I know you can't find one who would go back there for a salary, but they look at those waves and get all melancholy about their ancestors. Down here, they even bury their dead along the riverbanks, facing east, too, and won't ever go back to the cemetery til it's time to plant somebody else.

"Come on, Miss Althea," Daddy said, "I got a good looking colored man I want you to meet."

Miss Althea leaned over the stove and jabbed the fork into a piece of chicken. The juice set the grease to popping. She cocked her head in Daddy's direction. "How you talk, Mr. Mac, why-fo you think I needs me a man."

Daddy kept it up. "Why, I figgered you'd about wore that ol' Willie Simmons slap out."

She laughed and slapped herself on the thigh with the flat of the fork. She was three hundred pounds if she was an ounce, old Willie about half that. "Who that man you talkin' 'bout?"

Daddy got this evil grin. "Let's see now...what was his name?" He turned to me.

"Henry Manigault," I said.

Miss Althea jabbed at the chicken again, began forking it onto last week's *Palmetto Post*. A picture of Benito Mussolini soaked up the grease. Her face went blank while she turned the name over in her mind.

And then she figured it out. "Oooh, Lawd!" she hollered. "Great God, Mr. Mac, why you trouble this ol' woman so?" She heaped the chicken into the basket with the deviled eggs and the white bread and the jar of tea, then slapped down the lid and shoved the basket at Daddy. "Get out of this kitchen all two both of you! Get on from heah!"

And she flapped her apron at us and ran us right out onto the back porch like we was stray dogs that had somehow snuck into the house.

Chapter Twelve

I don't know if Miss Althea thought we was fooling or not. But when we got to Dr. Indigo's, there he was, waiting on his front step. Daddy hadn't called him, 'cause he had no phone.

And he was a sight, too. All gankey, you know what I mean, walking to the truck like he was bucking a forty knot gale. He had on pants a couple of sizes too big, a loose long-sleeved white shirt, a copper bracelet on one wrist, a broad brimmed straw hat tied down with a red bandana, and of course, those blue glasses. Daddy had his on, too.

Dr. Indigo had his snake-head cane in one hand, a paper A & P bag in the other. Halfway to the truck, he stopped, poked at something on the ground, bent over and dropped it in the bag. Lord knows what it was. Then he straightened up as best he could and worked his way across the yard, slow and royal, like he was the Last King of the Yorubas who died about the time Columbus thought he found India.

Dr. Indigo made it to the door and then there arose a question of etiquette. In those days, if you picked up a Negro, he rode in the back. If you picked up a white man, the youngest man would get out and ride in the wind and let the older man sit down. But here we had one old Negro and one hog-cut white boy.

I was wondering what I should do, but Daddy sorted it out pretty quick. "Get in the back, bub, and let Mr. Henry sit down."

Daddy never called him Dr. Indigo. And he never called him Mr. Manigault, either. You can bet I called him "Mr. Henry" and "sir" the few times I spoke to him. He called me "boy" and Daddy "Sheriff."

I opened the door and got the crutches onto the ground and slid out and hobbled around to the tailgate. Daddy had hosed out most of the blood, but you could still see a drop here and there, all dried-up and looking like that old lead paint we used to slap on the bottoms of our boats to keep down the barnacles and seagrass.

I slid up right behind the cab to get out of the roadwind and kept my mind on the scenery as we rolled across the islands down to the sea, past the fields and pastures and blue-door shanties, past graveyards with the stones all facing east, past churches and juke joints, just starting to draw crowds this sunny July Saturday.

It was just like you took your best friend's woman on a ride clear across the county. You might have just gone fishing, but you might have just as well took your britches off from the way some people would talk. The Negroes walking along the road all saw us. So did the white people in cars. And what a sight we must have been. The sheriff in his blue glasses, the water-walking doctor in his, the healed-up boy in the back. Let me tell you, we couldn't have done much better with a brass band in the Decoration Day parade. Daddy was in.

Well, he was and he wasn't and I'll get to that after a bit. We drove while the oaks got smaller and then played out altogether. And then the pines took over and by the time you could see the ocean shimmering off in the distance, there was just cassina, wax myrtle, and cedar, all stunted from the salt air. Then there was nothing but sea oats and beach grass and the blue water beyond.

There was a rutted trail through the dunes to the hard-packed beach. Daddy downshifted and hung his head out the window and hollered, "Hold on, son."

I did and it was a rough ride. I cracked my head on the back of the cab and licked my lips just when he cleared a bump and bit my tongue til it welled but didn't bleed. We got through the worst of it, and eased down the beach half a mile, or so. Then Daddy pulled over to where the sea had broke through the dunes and rolled way back into the woods. There was shade there, and a world of flotsom, net floats and timbers and bits of line and a life jacket that said *Eli Whitney*.

Daddy spotted it first. He picked it up and turned it over and gave it to Mr. Henry without saying anything. And Mr. Henry closed his eyes and ran his hands over it and said, "He make the cotton gin."

Well, how he knew that is beyond me. All I knew was *Eli Whitney* was sunk by the Germans and they were probably out there right now, spying on us. Years later I learned how Eli

Whitney had him a rich widow and she kept him on her plantation right down past Savannah. And how he saw the slaves picking out cotton seeds by hand and he invented the gin and pretty soon everybody wanted more slaves to grow more cotton to keep the gins busy. And then that old bastard went and made parts for muskets that slaughtered half a million men in the war he helped cause. He was damn near as bad as Sherman, the way I figure it.

Anyway, Daddy put the life jacket in the back of the truck, dropped the tailgate and grabbed the basket out of the cab. Miss Althea had done us right, as she generally did, with a white linen tablecloth and napkins rolled up just so. Her chicken was the way it always was, enough to make a man jump up and down and holler.

Or course, I wasn't doing any jumping up and down. I sat there, my bum leg propped on a palmetto stump, and we ate the chicken and the deviled eggs and washed it down with tea dark as Little Glory headwater. That life jacket had sort of taken the steam out of us, as you might imagine, and we ate without speaking. Mr. Henry had come up short a few teeth over the years, mostly in front, and both of us got through long before he did. We sat there and watched him, me about to bust from the questions I couldn't ask, Daddy from the ones he wouldn't, and Mr. Henry just mouthing Miss Althea's chicken like he did everything else, real slow.

We watched him and he watched us and I saw our reflections in his blue glasses and you could have cut the air with a knife.

Then Mr. Henry put down his chicken leg, bent over like it

was paining him and picked up this big old conch laying in the tidewash. He shook the sand out of it and pressed it to his ear and said, "Hello."

Mr. Henry paused and I looked for something in his face, a flutter of a cheek, an eyelid. All I saw was blue glass.

"Yessir." He nodded like Daddy did, like most everybody did the first forty years we had phones. Then he turned to Daddy and held out the shell. "It's for you," he said.

Daddy took the shell, and from that second on, he was bound for glory. That's what I was about to tell you awhile back. All the Negroes said Daddy had the power. All but one.

Daddy looked at the shell to make sure no hermit crab would come out and nip him, then he put it to his ear. "Hello," he said. "Hello?" Then after ten seconds or so, he turned to Mr. Henry. "I feel like a damn fool."

Mr. Henry was smiling like an undertaker does when he slips you the bill. "What you hear, Sheriff?"

Daddy gave the shell back. "Just the sea, like when I was a boy."

"That sea bring us all heah," he said. Then he put the shell to his ear again. "Yessir, he here all right. Nossir, he can't talk now. You call him back, you hear? Goodbye. Yessir, yessir. Goodbye."

Mr. Henry eased the shell back where he found it, slowly straighted up and looked Daddy square in the eye. "Listen here, Mr. Mac McCloud, I ain't long. You look after my people."

Daddy bowed up. "I'm the law, Mr. Henry, I got to look after all the people."

Mr. Henry snorted. "White people don't need no looking after." He raised his chin and if it weren't for those glasses, I'd a swore the old man was crying. But when he spoke again, his voice was steady, soft, and low. "This ol' war gonna last a while. Gonna be a lot of folks goin' where they don't want to go. But not that boy. He be just fine."

"Mr. Henry," Daddy says, "I don't know how you did it, but...."

Old Indigo shushed him with a wave of his hand. "That don't matter. I got the power and I use 'em. What you gone do?"

Daddy sat on the edge of the tailgate and held his hands between his knees like a school kid fessing up. He looked off into middle distance. "Mr. Henry, I don't know what to call it. How can I know what I got."

Dr. Indigo chuckled. "You ain't got to call 'em."

"What you call 'em, Mr. Henry?"

"I ain't know what to call 'em, either."

That's the way Old Indigo was. He never give you much, and what he did was slippery as a garfish. And that's the way the rest of the day went, blue glasses flashing in the sun and Daddy and the doctor lubing up the language, each wanting more, neither coming clean.

And I didn't dare say a thing.

Miss Althea had gone on home by the time we got home. I sat at the kitchen table while Daddy made me fresh tomato sandwiches, you know where you lift and eat fast before they fall through the crust. I had two or three, then crawled off to bed. Boy, I was bushed, my first time out of the house in two weeks. My head hit the pillow and I was gone.

But long about midnight, I heard something rattle off the screen, a big old June bug, or a luna moth or maybe a bat. There were lots of bats around summertimes. They'd hide out beneath the roof shakes during daylight, aggravate a person in the evenings, hanging off the eaves clicking and chirping, and sometimes come rattling down the chimney and bust loose in the kitchen and send Miss Althea screaming and hollering out into the yard. I'd shoo them outside with the broom or swat them with the *Palmetto Post*, and since Miss Althea was way too heavy for the step ladder, get the Spic and Span and clean up the chimney soot they left on the plaster wherever they bounced off the walls. Daddy said it was good to have them around, since they ate up so many bugs, but I'd rather have the skeeters any day.

I was half awake, thinking about them bats, when, *vip*, there it went again. Then I head Harley Davidson whisper, "Mr. Lil Mac, Mr. Lil Mac."

My bed was close to the window so I could catch the breeze off the river, it being so blistering hot that summer. I rolled over, grabbed the sill and hauled myself over and put my nose to the screen. It was a full moon that night and there he was, out in the yard, ready to throw another pinecone at my window. "Harley Davidson," I whispered, "what in the devil are you doing out so late?"

"I done been on patrol," he whispered back, "you know, blackout patrol."

"Yeah?" I said. "That's good."

"Naw sir, Mr. Lil Mac, it warn't good."

"What you mean? I told you that man said little chillern was a dying over there and we got to do what we could."

"Yessir, I knows that. I done what I could."

"You see any lights?"

"Yessir."

"You make 'em shut 'em off?"

There was a long pause. "Naw, sir."

"Well, why in the hell not?"

Harley Davidson stood on one foot and then the other, like he had to pee real bad. "There was candles all around and the window wide open. She was a-laying in the bathtub washin' herself and a-hollering out for Jesus!"

"Damn it all, Harley. First it was two German submarines..."

"Naw sir, Mr. Lil Mac, this here the truth." He called it "trute" like all the Negroes did.

"Who?" I asked.

"Squinchy new gal," he said.

This didn't seem right to me, so I said: "You mean Miss Marzette was singing hymns and taking a bath. Why Harley Davidson, what's wrong with you, looking in a white woman's window? Daddy will arrest you for that."

"Oh Lordy, Mr. Lil Mac! I ain't want to look, but I just had to!" He paused for a couple of seconds. "One of them Germans could a shot a tornado at her and blowed her all to maternity."

I tried to tell him that *tornadoes* flew through the air but *torpedoes* didn't, but he just wouldn't listen. That's the way he always was. He'd get in a particular frame of mind and you'll play hell trying to change it. But, then, he was only ten years old and he just saw a redheaded woman naked, so I guess you can't hardly blame him.

We whispered back and forth. "Naw sir, Mr. Lil Mac, she warn't singing no hymns. She was a-washin' herself and moanin' and a-hollerin' for Jesus, just like I said."

"Well, of course she was washin' herself. How else is a woman gonna take a bath?"

"Oh, Lordy, Mr. Lil Mac! Oh, Lordy."

"What, Harley, what?"

"Not herself, Mr. Lil Mac, *herself*," he pointed to his britches, "down there!"

"What you say?"

"Yessir, yessir, with this funny little red rag. For a long time, too. She ought to be real clean now."

Well, I didn't know what to make of it, so I sent him off to bed. He took a few steps, then turned and asked: "You ain't gonna tell you daddy?"

"No, I ain't. But next time you see a light, you go 'round and knock on the door and get them to turn it off. You hear?"

"Well, Mr. Lil Mac, I would-a, but I just couldn't get no gumption."

"And don't you go sneakin' 'round to white women's windows."

He shook his head solemnly. "Naw sir, I ain't never gone do that again. Tornadoes, or no."

"Good night. Get some sleep."

"Yessir, Mr. Lil Mac, I'll try."

He waved and walked away and I slid myself back square in the bed again. Way out over the Little Glory, the moon was a-coasting along amongst the clouds, sailing on a silver sea. The wind come ghosting up from the river, and somewhere out in the rice fields, a lonesome old bull gator bellered.

Chapter Thirteen

There was two types of Negroes in Albemarle in those days: those who had white folks, and those who didn't. The ones who didn't kinda scraped along as best they could. But if you had a good field hand or a good cook or a boatman or a huntmaster, you just didn't have them, but you had most of their relatives, too. After a dozen years, or so, you all got to love one another, and were thick as kin. You'd give them clothes and venison and pay their doctor and bail them out of jail. They'd bring you huckleberries and butter beans and mullet and name their children after you. The relationship was hereditary and transferable. Forty years later, a Negro down on his luck could remind you that his great aunt used to take care of your grandmother and your neighbors would think poorly of you if you did not meet your obligations. Miss Althea had her white folks and damned if she was going to give them up to a little snip of a redheaded girl.

They waltzed around the kitchen like a couple of scorpions, Miss Althea and Miss Marzette, trying to kill each other with niceties. Miss Althea had cooked the ham and the yams and Miss Marzette had brought the biscuits. But Miss Althea's biscuits were famous, big as a cat head and layered like fine French pastry. You could pour beans over them or sop them in your gravy, and if you saved one or two, you could drizzle on Brer Rabbit Pure Cane Syrup for desert. They were a great pride to her and she didn't take to nobody else's, specially in her own kitchen.

The ham was the last of the boar Daddy shot off me when it opened my leg and tried to eat my face. Daddy had gutted it and gave it to Willie Simmons and he cured it in an old phone booth he used for a smokehouse. The glass was black as midnight and the gaskets burnt off the door, but the Southern Bell sign was still on top and the phone was in there, too, but it didn't work anymore. Anyway, Willie smoked the boar and gave us back half. It was quite a while before I could bring myself to eat any, but after I got over that, it was pretty good, especially all stuck full of cloves and plastered with brown sugar and mustard.

This all come about in early spring of 1943, just after the government man stopped Daddy out on the highway and told him he had been drafted into the service of the United States.

I had turned ten and was off my crutches but still gimping some. Meanwhile, the war had drug on and got a whole lot meaner. Old Hitler was trying to whip the British and the supplies we was sending them was just barely keeping them going. The ships would covey up in New York harbor and the navy would escort them across the ocean. But they had to get to New York first. They come straggling up the coast in twos and threes, hauling gasoline from Houston and sugar from Cuba and bullets from Biloxi and the Germans would lay for them and sink them if they could.

The list of ships that went down was a long one and I forget most of them. There was the *Eliza Lucas, Bahama Star,* and *Marine Sulphur Queen,* which went up like a big firecracker and left not a man alive to tell the tale. All through the winter of '42 and '43 the wind washed the war onto our beaches—the greasy slicks, the splintered oars, the holed lifeboats, and the sad and empty life jackets with the names of ships nobody remembers. And then the government put a mounted patrol on every island from New Jersey to Florida.

Daddy brought the news one Thursday evening, about the time Miss Althea was heading home. I was upstairs washing up when there came a rattling on the bathroom door. "Daddy?" I said.

But it was Miss Althea. "You got your britches on, chile?"

"Yassum."

She opened the door. "You daddy home. He want a leetle compersation."

I wondered if he found out that me and Harley Davidson had stole those boards off the back of the chicken coop. The mink and coon had gotten after the birds so bad we had given up raising them, and the coop just stood there empty and forlorn, with glass busted out and the fennel high as the windowsills. Now that I was better, I was an Official Junior Blackout Compliance Warden again. I demoted Harley Davidson to deputy, and we snuck around back, peeled off the siding, and spiked it together in the crown of an oak about a quarter mile down the river. Way up there, we'd pull double duty, we figured, looking for lights and spotting enemy planes, which is what I wanted to do in the first place. But we were short on equipment. No photos of military aircraft, no I-D chart, no altitude height finder, no flight direction indicator, logbook, armband, or metal sign to nail on our live oak tree. After school one day, Harley and I sat down and wrote a letter to Franklin Delano Roosevelt about it, but he never wrote back.

But right then I figured he did, and Daddy had got the letter and found out about the coop and the nails in his oak and he was either going to hug me or whup my fanny and I'd find out which the minute I seen his face. But no, it was the government man in the dark green car with flashing lights hid behind the grill, stopping the sheriff of Calhoun County and putting papers in his hand like he was wanted by the law.

Well, I guess Daddy was wanted by the law, if you call the government the law and it thinks you ought to, even if it don't deserve it some times. But that didn't matter right then. There was a war on and Daddy had papers in his hand and he had to go. I'd heard it a hundred times, but this time there would be no argument.

There would be two dozen men riding the beaches from the mouth of the Little Glory to the Georgia line. They would camp in beach shacks and ride the dunes and watch the sea. They would need ham and beans and biscuits and hay for their horses. They would need somebody to send them out and bring them in and fill out the forms. Daddy knew his river. He knew the big creeks and the little creeks and the mudflats where the tide eddied and swirled. He knew the islands and the little hummocks and the green marsh from here to Jericho. Daddy would command them. Maybe he couldn't do a God's thing to help those poor men at sea, but if them Germans wanted to get ashore, they'd have to get past him. I wondered if they knew he was bulletproof.

"I maybe have to get me a horse," he said.

"A hoss?" Miss Althea said. "Maybe git you a mule."

We were in the kitchen and the rifle and the uniform the government man had gave him were laid out on the table. It was all left over from the last war, leggings and funny little puttee britches, and a tin hat like a barber's washbasin. Daddy was studying the papers. "It don't say if it's my horse or theirs."

"Got to be theirs," I said. "They wouldn't make you bring your own." I was eyeing the rifle. It was a Springfield, as I remember, Model of 1903. "Can I touch it?"

"You know what you got to do first?"

I knew that ever since he gave me my pellet rifle. "Make sure it's unloaded?"

"Yep."

He picked it up and worked the bolt and passed it to me. I didn't see any bullets, so I closed the action and tried to bring it to my shoulder but it was way too heavy. I gave it back. "This would kill a hog," I said. "Could you kill you a German with it?"

Daddy smiled sort of sad. "I hope I don't have to kill nobody. But I gotta go out there and do what I can."

"Uh," Miss Althea said. "That sho nuff a shame. Who gone tek care of this boy evenin's?"

"I was thinking about asking Miss Marzette."

Miss Althea got all twiss-mout. "Who?"

"Mr. Elmore's new gal." Daddy paused only a second, but there was an eternity hiding in it. Then he said, "The redhead."

Miss Althea grunted. "That young gal need tek care of she-shelf."

So that's how those two women got to stirring round the kitchen together, rattling the pots and shuffling dishes and Yes Ma'aming each other nearly to death. Then Miss Marzette called us to the table. Miss Althea did not like that either and she snorted and went to beller up Harley Davidson.

Daddy and I sat down and Miss Marzette brought the ham and Miss Althea the yams and a big bowl of fried okra. And then Miss Althea and Harley got their plates and pulled up to the little table next to the stove like they always did. Me and Daddy was about to dig in when Miss Marzette said, "Mac, aren't you forgettin' something?"

I suppose Daddy prayed when that Negro took a shot at him in the Swing Low Sweet Juke Joint, and a couple of other times, too, but he didn't go pestering God all the time. He put down his fork. "Sorry. Say the grace, bub."

I tucked my head, but Miss Marzette shut me down. "Why Mac, I'm surprised at you. How can you even think of praying to God when the one who cooked your supper ain't even allowed at this table?"

Daddy cut his eyes at her. "What you mean, Marzette? I didn't know you got religion."

Miss Marzette's eyes flashed. "I go to the Free Will, Free Love Baptist Church, thank you Mr. McCloud, and we believe all of us are made in the image of the Lord."

"Well, Miz Roosevelt," Daddy said, "would you like me to ask them to join us?"

Daddy could have just as well left Eleanor Roosevelt out of it. The food was getting cold.

Miss Marzette drew up her mouth til it looked like one of those little pop open coin purses. "Why thank you, Mr. McCloud, I do vote Democrat." She slid back her chair and stood up. "And I think tonight, I will be voting with my feet."

Daddy jumped up so fast, he knocked over his chair. He reached for her hand, but she snatched it away from him. "I'm sorry, Marzette, I don't know what got into me. Sit down, please sit back down."

I guess it never occured to Miss Marzette that Miss Athea and Harley Davidson might not want to sit here and watch us buckra faces mouth our vittles. In a boat or on the ground or out in the woods, everybody just spread out and got comfortable as they could and ate sandwiches or passed around the lard bucket full of perlow or gumbo or slum-gullion. But inside, Negroes and whites never ate together. If those Freedom Riders would have figured that out, they would have been Freedom Feeders instead. They could have taken some of that Democrat money and throwed a feedin' on the ground and everybody would have come and the segregated lunch counters would have lost business and there would have been a whole lot less trouble. But it was just like that Charleston planter who wouldn't let his redheaded daughter marry Sherman.

Right then, Daddy had his own redhead to worry about.

Miss Marzette just stood there pouting. My, but she was a pretty thing. All fired up the way redheads do, Daddy didn't stand a chance. "I'm sorry," he said again. "Would you like me to have them join us?"

"No, Mac, I would not like to have you tell them to join us. I'd like you to ask them."

I reckon that's when I started learning about women. Not only wouldn't Miss Marzette slack off an inch, she took up slack she didn't have. Well, I reckon she had plenty of slack, like women always do, sittin' on what they're sittin' on. Of course, I was only ten and didn't know too much about all that then, but I was catching on, thanks to Harley Davidson being an Official Junior Blackout Compliance Warden.

So Daddy went into the kitchen and Miss Marzette sat back down. There was some *compersation* back there I didn't quite catch, then Harley and Miss Althea come out hauling their plates, Harley with this hang-dog look, Miss Althea puckering her lips and rolling her eyes.

They all sat down and I finally got to say the blessing, the old one I learned at my momma's church, the Church of the Cross. "Lord, for what we are about to receive, make us truly thankful for all our many blessings...." It was short and to the point and included a line for all the hungry people from the Chinese to the Armenians.

And then the platters went around. We had about all got dished up, and Miss Althea was hunkering down and figured she was going to actually eat with white folks when Miss Marzette jumped up again. "Oh sweet Lord," she said, cussing as easy as a woman can cuss, "I forgot the biscuits."

Miss Althea snorted again and Miss Marzette scurried off to fetch them and came back to the table with a quarter peck sweetgrass basket loaded up with biscuits the size of doorknobs, tucked into a red dishtowel to keep them warm. Miss Marzette passed them to Daddy first and he took two, then to Miss Althea who eyed them skeptical and took one.

The basket was coming my way when I caught Harley Davidson out of the corner of one eye. He had stopped chewing. A long string of ham fat hung from his lips, swinging like a pendulum. And he was watching that basket like he'd seen a big old cockroach peek out from under a biscuit. Then he covered his mouth and started to cough, weak and phony at first, then deeper and more genuine with each breath.

Miss Althea cut her eyes at him. "Boy, you eat like I ain't feed you in a week. You gone kill you self less you chew them vittle."

Harley kept it up, then excused himself from the table. We could hear him off in the kitchen, hacking and wheezing like he had a mullet bone cross-wise in his throat. "Land sakes," Miss Marzette said, "what ails that boy?"

Well, I knew something was up. "I'll draw him some water," I said and followed him into the kitchen.

He was over by the cook stove, wild-eyed and just greasy with sweat. "It's that rag," he said.

"What rag?"

"You know, Mr. Lil Mac, that rag."

"No, I don't. What rag you talkin' 'bout?"

"Oh Lordy, Mr. Lil Mac. The one she was a-washin' herself with."

"No!"

"Yessir, it sure is. And I wouldn't eat none of them biscuits if I was you."

I looked back into the dining room. Daddy was halfway through his second.

Chapter Fourteen

Well, first he was bulletproof, then he got The Sight, and now Daddy was hoodooed by a redhead. Maybe Miss Marzette had enough magic of her own, but the hoodoo clinched the nail, if you know what I mean. She laid spread legged in a bathtub on the full moon, poured some special root doctor dope in the water, lit seven candles, prayed and washed herself way down there for a good long time and then dried out the rag and served her man biscuits in it. It's a killer and it works every time.

I don't suppose I have to tell you she was the white woman Samuel Dibble saw at Dr. Indigo's, but I will, just in case you missed it. Maybe you think it's strange that a member of the Free Will, Free Love Baptist Church would do such a thing. Well, maybe it's not something you'd run bragging to your preacher about, but the lines ain't cut quite that clean down here. It's damn near like New Orleans, where the French Quarter Catholics carry a rosary in one pocket and a chicken foot in the other. And besides, Miss Marzette was a redhead and she was in love and love will make a redheaded woman do fool things.

And if that weren't enough, Daddy had got himself drafted.

I know you might be saying Lil Mac is just talking Southern and his daddy got drafted. But he got himself drafted. He pestered the commander of the Fifth Naval District about Sam Dibble's submarine and turned in that life jacket off the *Eli Whitney*. So, when the government decided to trot out the pony patrol and they needed somebody to lead them, Daddy's name was fresh in their minds and, hoodoo or not, he had to go. Bodine got to be acting sheriff, just like Harley Davidson was Acting Official Junior Blackout Compliance Warden while I was hog-cut and laid up. And I got to be acting deputy sheriff.

Well, not really, but I liked to think I was. I dug Daddy's badge out of his dresser top drawer, laid it on a piece of gold poster board I swiped from school, and cut out one just like his and pinned it to my shirts. I hung around the office, answered the phone and went for the mail and did whatever other errands needed to be done, if they could be done on foot and didn't have to be done in no hurry. When we'd drive the squad car down to Lonnie Mulligan's, Bodine would let me pump the gas and check the oil and air up the tires. Of course, whenever we had the chance, me and Harley kept up with our air raid and blackout work, but it was pretty drearisome and nothing come of it for months and months.

But that was after we sent Daddy off to war. Bodine and Miss Marzette and me, on the city dock one drizzly Monday morning, when the sea fog come a-rolling in over the islands like you'd roll out a wet gray rug, muffling everything but the sad old horns of the ships at sea worrying their way north to New York. Ah-who-gah, ah-who-gah, a blast every two minutes, so low you could feel them even if you could not hear. The river was the color of the sky, of the air, slick as axle grease, and the gulls and pelicans and the po-joes just sat there on the dock pilings, too disgusted to even fly.

Daddy had on his leftovers from the Great War, the puttee britches, tight at waist, knee, and fanny, all floppy everywhere else, brogans and leggings, his tin hat, and a khaki shirt bearing the bright silver bars of a First Lieutenant. The rifle and two bandoliers hung from his shoulders, stinking like old ammunition does, like ammonia and old brass. Miss Marzette sat on his duffle bag and leaned her head against the point of his hip, her eyes swole up with tears.

I was 'bout to cry, myself. Was I proud of him? Lordy, I was. But he was all I had and I didn't want to let him go. Old Indigo had said I would be all right and Daddy would be all right, and I wanted to believe it but I got him a little help, anyway. I snuck out of bed the night before, when Daddy was snoring like a dull saw gnawing at a rotten board, eased the door open and slipped out to the shed. There on a shelf above the cast nets and bait buckets was half a can of blue paint. It was hant blue, you know, the same shade the Negroes paint their door and window frames to keep back the spirits.

I found a brush and came back inside and bent the hell out of two of Miss Althea's butter knives getting the can open. I would have wrote it on the back of his government shirt; hell, I would have wrote it on his forehead, but that wouldn't have stopped him from getting shot in the back and the *Palmetto Post* said the Germans did that a lot. So I went rummaging through the ragbag and found what was left of that sheet Miss Althea used to bind my foot when I sliced it on that shell when I thought Daddy was going to take me fishing.

I cut a broad swatch of cloth, long enough to wrap clean around his chest. I daubed and wrote "bulletproof" once for the front, once for the back. I didn't know any German so I hoped at least one of them was smart enough to know English.

Daddy found it in the morning and laughed and hugged me and rolled it up and stuck it in his pocket and I believe if he hadn't been the sheriff of Calhoun County, he would have busted out bawling. He was all I had, too, except Miss Marzette.

So there we were on the dock, waiting on a boat I hoped would not come. Maybe we would wait awhile and then I would go back to school, and when I got home, Miss Althea would make me dinner and long about sunset, Daddy would come rattling up the drive. And then, after Miss Althea went on home, Daddy would go pick up Miss Marzette and he would tell his stories on the Little Glory front porch and the moon would come up over the river like it always did and Miss Marzette would tuck me into bed, like she had lately taken to doing. But after awhile, we heard the rattle of a diesel and Auxiliary River Patrol Craft 706 loomed up out of the mist.

Seven-O-Six used to be the Tammy Jane, a forty foot shrimper of Georgia pine, pulling her nets off Tybee Island. Before the war she made her skipper a pretty good living off the shrimp and mullet and flounder he sold at the city market in Savannah, but the government snagged him and sent him off to the South Pacific and by and by we saw his name in the

Palmetto Post, killed in action on some God-forsaken island whose name I wouldn't spell even if I could remember it. Then the government bought the boat from the skipper's widow, slobbered gray paint all over her lovely lines, tore off the outriggers, and put on a boom for handling freight. They rigged her with a radio and a flag and a machine gun, which was about as ornamental as the flag, specially if she ran into a German sub.

The swabbie at the helm backed her down and nudged her against the dock and Daddy picked up his duffel and stepped aboard. Miss Marzette leaned over and gave him one last kiss, then the swabbie threw her into reverse and the water between the boat and the dock got wider and wider until they couldn't kiss no more. And then Auxiliary River Patrol Craft 706 rattled away into that forever of fog. Daddy pulled the banner from his pocket and held it up and grinned. Bulletproof. He had on his blue glasses, too.

And then Miss Marzette looked at me with them slitty little red eyes and gave me a hug and said she would be out at Little Glory right after work. And Bodine said he would drop me off at school and pick me up when it was over and I could help him police the county. And I did, too.

It all went pretty well until the riot. There had been some mumbling amongst the Negroes that year. Hitler was hanging on and Tojo hanging tough and the first and third Monday of each month men were rolling out of Albemarle on Southwind motor coaches and a lot of them would come back in boxes or not at all. They were mostly Negroes. Of course, Negroes couldn't be officers. They couldn't drive tanks or run ships. Oh, they let a few of them fly towards the end of the war, and they got pretty good at it, as you might expect. But most of them just drove trucks or handled freight or dug ditches. I don't reckon that was as bad as what the Yankees did, throwing Negro infantry into the hottest fights, but in December of 1944, it didn't make much of difference. The weather had soured and the planes couldn't fly and the Germans counter-attacked on the Belgian border at a place they called the Bulge. Will Mahoney ran the headlines in twenty-eight point type: *Square Head Germans Machine Gun Negroes.*

First off, I didn't know what to make of it. We all knew the Germans had square heads. I thought the Army had give the Negroes machine guns and I wondered why Will Mahoney would have a problem with that. But then I read on down a bit and got the straight skinny. The Germans had captured a bunch of our Negroes and figured they weren't worth the groceries it'd take to keep them and lined them up and shot down a hundred or so.

Well, I might have misread it, but the Calhoun County Negroes did not. At least the ones who could read, anyway.

And then all hell broke loose.

Bodine was pulling his Monday morning wee hour duty, making sure all the draftees got on board. They got through the roll call all right, but when it came time to get on the bus, they balked. Bodine tried to get them moving, but it was like herding cats. And then they began to sing:

> *Gonna lay down my burden,*
> *Down by the river side,*
> *Down by the river side,*

Down by the river side,
Gonna lay down my burden,
Down by the river side,
Ain't gonna study war no mo'.

Bodine picked the Negro with the sweetest voice and laid into him with the billy-club and the rest of the Negroes jumped in and they had them a battle royal right there on Boundary Street, a great pile of hollering and kicking and gouging Negroes with Bodine on the bottom. If that ox of a Negro sergeant hadn't come boiling out of the bus and pistol-whipped a couple of men on top, they would have killed him for sure.

As it was, all he lost was his badge, which was a lot to lose, in more ways than one, which I'll get to after awhile. I saw him after I got loose from school, pretty well used up and still riled as a banty rooster.

"Lil Mac," he said, "where's your pappy's badge?"

"In his dresser," I said. "Right where Daddy left it."

There was a big hole in his shirt where his used to be. "I'll need to borry it til I get me a new one."

Well, Bodine was Acting Sheriff and Daddy's badge said Sheriff and I wasn't about to let him have it. "I'll see if I can dig it out," I said.

Bodine cocked his eye at me, and all at once I could see what the Negroes hated. And I knew right then, he had killed Bo Manigualt. And here I was, a boy with a bum leg, about to lock horns with a murderer. "You said it was right in his dresser."

I had to think fast. "Yessir, less Miss Athea moved it."

"I don't reckon Miss Althea's got any business pawing

through your daddy's things."

You heard of being saved by the bell? Well, I was saved by Southern Bell.

Bodine walked to the phone. "Sheriff's Department," he said, "Sheriff Jim Bodine speaking." He listened a while, nodded and then cussed. "All of 'em?" he said. "Every single one?" Then he cussed some more. "I'll have to notify Mac McCloud."

"What?" I asked after he hung up.

"Seems like we just sent the Army a whole busload of niggers with heart murmurs."

Chapter Fifteen

That's how Daddy got sent home early. But it wasn't really early; it was late. By then, we had them Germans sucking wind and what few subs they had left was bunched up on the other side of the sea, bothering folks there instead of here. But the government had got started late with the pony patrol and, by God, they were gonna ride her out to the very end. And who knows, the flat-face Japs could have snuck over from the Pacific Ocean, just to throw us off.

But they didn't. Daddy was out there a year and a damn month and other than a sunk lifeboat with a single dead man in it and a few plumes way out to sea, he seen nothing but gulls and porpoises, floppy eared does, the rag-horned island bucks, a possum or two, some sea turtles, and upwards of a thousand coons. He got leave a couple of times, but those few days he come ashore, between me and Miss Marzette, there just wasn't enough of him to go around.

Meanwhile, I had got real fond of Miss Marzette. She was off a farm in Hampton County and she knew the most wonderful things, like which flowers fetched up the butterflies and why the moon was an hour later each night and how you make an Injun lamp out of a jar of lightning bugs. She deviled Willie Simmons into plowing up the chicken yard and we got us a garden in the ground, with melons and punkins big as boulders and sugar cane and corn taller than a man can reach and marigolds all round to keep back the tater beetles. Even Miss Althea warmed up to her some, once she figured she wasn't out to steal her white folks.

Miss Marzette kept patches on my britches and buttons on my shirts and got me to saying grace before each meal. She helped me with my reading, which was none too good, but instead of my school book, she had me read from tracts from that Free Will, Free Love bunch called "Why Do the Heathen Rage?"

I jumped right on the first one, since I thought it would be giving that damn Hitler hell, but there wasn't nothing about him in there at all, just a bunch of stuff about seven-headed beasts and the dark of the moon and blood as deep as horses' stirrups and the Great Whore, but it never said who she was. I would have asked Miss Marzette, but it was just too embarrassing.

She worked me hard on my writing, too, which wasn't much better than I could read. Back before Miss Marzette, Miss Althea said "Boy, you ambidex. You ain't do a ting with all-two-boff hands." But that wasn't true. I was left-handed in a right-handed world and I smeared the ink when I drug my wrist across everything I wrote. When I held my wrist off the paper, my elbow took over and the letters all kind of ran together and looked the same. You couldn't tell *hold* from *hell* or *buck* from some other word that rhymes with it, and I was catching the devil about it at school.

Miss Marzette figured to cure me and sat me down with a Bible and pen and a stack of paper and told me to pick out a verse and write it a hundred times. She suggested something like John 3:16 "For God so loved the world that he gave his only begotten Son so that all should not perish but have Everlasting Life." But that was too tedious for pen or consideration, specially the Everlasting Life part, since a man who is old and sick ought to be able to lay down and expect some rest.

Then she come up with something out of First Corinthians about love being better than faith and hope. I liked that a little better, but it was still too long, so I fanned through the whole thing, from Genesis to Revelation. I come across something in the Song of Solomon, where it said "Thy navel is a goblet that needeth not wine." I liked it, but I didn't know why, and figured on writing it, but it got me to thinking about the story Harley Davidson told about Miss Marzette in the bathtub a-hollering out for Jesus, so I let that one go, too. Then in Matthew I found the perfect verse in the story where Jesus tarried when he was off cross-country to see a buddy who had took sick and died before Jesus got there.

So I wrote "Jesus wept" a hundred times and gave it to Miss Marzette and she got kind of snippish and said she hoped I had to read a lot of the book before I found it. At the time, I figured I was getting away with something, but let me tell you, I wish to hell I had written something about navels and love instead. I seen all this trouble we got and I seen Jesus weeping for the rest of my days and it gets terrible drearisome at times.

And Bodine? You can bet I stayed clear of him til Daddy got home. Right after Bo Manigualt turned up dead, Bodine kind of withered, but the licking he got under that pile of Negroes put the snort right back into him. It was kinda like watering a pine tree with turpentine. The meaner he got treated, the meaner he got. His stingereed hand had healed up and there was hell to pay, cracked heads all over Calhoun County, from Goldie's Blue Room to the parking lot behind the Cedar Grove sundown store, where the Negroes gathered on Friday nights and sat around beneath the oaks sucking on half pints of Old Setter. An Old Setter hangover was rough, but at least it didn't bleed like a Bodine hangover did.

It took a month for the Federal men to get ahold of the Army and for the Army to get ahold of the Fifth Naval District and probably the Coast Guard, too. But they finally had a pow-wow and got it straightened out and one Thursday in the early spring of 1945 when the camellias were busting with buds, Auxiliary River Patrol Craft 706 come a-rattling up the Little Glory River, its flag snapping and the sun glinting off that pitiful single machinegun.

Daddy was thinner and tanner and all that squinting through binoculars had give him little spiderwebs of wrinkles at the corners of his eyes. But he looked good, anyway. He stepped up onto the dock and I grabbed ahold of him on one side and Miss Marzette on the other and we hung on til he could hardly get turned around to salute the flag when old Seven-O-Six pulled back into the sucking ebbtide.

Lordy, it was good to have him back. He didn't get shot at and he didn't have to shoot nobody and he only had to haul out that one dead body and he was used to that. And now there weren't no question about who was going to wear that badge.

Bodine had ordered up another one from the Law and Order Police Supply Company, clear off in Chicago, Illinois. His old one was silver, but this one was gold and it had crossed billy sticks on the top and handcuffs on the bottom and his name wrote in between. But he ordered it before Daddy came home and it was slow coming and it said Acting Sheriff. Daddy made him put tape over the *Acting* part and write in *Deputy* instead and the whole thing got to be a great embarrassment, specially after the Negroes took up calling him Buckra Tape. So he ordered another with the right words, but it got lost in the mail and that's when I figured something was up. But I'm getting ahead of myself, once again.

We picked up Daddy and drove out to Little Glory and Miss Althea slapped a special supper on the table, the first of the sweet peas and the second round of collards and the south end of a northbound deer Willie Simmons had jack-lighted right before Christmas. All of us sat at the table together like Miss Marzette wanted us to, except Willie Simmons who begged off sick so he wouldn't have to eat with Buckra. And the sun went down and the first of the bull gators opened up and the chuck-will's-widows answered back and the hoot owls said the last thirteen months was just a dream.

And then Miss Althea got after the dishes and Miss Marzette set me to my homework and she and Daddy jumped into the pickup and rattled off somewheres for an hour or so. Then they came back to the big house all lit up and she tucked me in and she and Daddy took off again.

I laid out of school the next day, and while Miss Marzette worked for Squinchy, me and Daddy went fishing. He didn't take me down the Little Glory to salt; he had seen enough of that for awhile. But we sat on the rice dike just below the big house and hammered the slab bream, one right after the other til Daddy cut his eyes at me sidewise and asked me how many I wanted to clean. I looked in the bucket and figured we had enough.

I scaled them with a kitchen spoon on a pine board behind the kitchen, butchered them and laid them in the sink for Miss Althea, who shook them in a shopping bag full of cornmeal and spices and popped them into a kettle of hot lard.

After a day or two of good groceries and catching up with Miss Marzette and me, Daddy figured it was time to get back down to business. The government sent him the names of all the Negroes who had turned up with heart murmurs. Daddy went down the list til he found somebody he knew, then laid for him one Saturday night in the bushes outside the Swing Low Sweet Juke Joint.

The boy come out just about Dead Time, which is what the Negroes call the first half hour of the new day, when all the spirits are out making mischief. One ghost will generally stay in the graveyard and call the rest back in at a quarter after four, so day-clean won't catch 'em. But in the meantime the plateyes and hags and jack-mullaters go roaming all over the countryside, giving decent people no peace.

Anyway, the boy come a-wobbling down the road, a-hanging on this gal nearly as drunk as he was, but they sobered up pretty quick when Daddy rizz up out of the broomsedge and fennel with the moon on those blue glasses.

'Course, I wasn't there to see any of this, but Daddy told me about it in the morning, the boy shaking and slobbering and the gal a-screaming "Oh Lawd! Oh Lawd!" with every breath. That boy gave up Exhibit A in a New York minute, a half pint flask with a half inch of hippity-hoppity heart juice still slopping around in the bottom of it. But when it came to answers, he locked up tight as Jonathan Polite. Daddy took him by the collar and shook him til his head bobbed and rolled like he was one of those little dogs in the back window of a Mexican's car. But it weren't no use. Caught between two root doctors, like that, he was struck dumb as an oak stump.

If he couldn't speak stone drunk there on the side of the road, he damn sure couldn't in court stone sober, so Daddy turned him loose and sent the jar off to the state lab in Columbia. We was waiting for them to get back to us when Bodine's badge finally turned up.

On Tuesday, I stopped by to see Daddy after school, and Bodine was at Daddy's desk, cussing to himself and digging at the engraving with his thumbnail. I spoke to him as polite as I could and went on out back to where Daddy was fighting a new fan belt onto the squad car.

"Afternoon, Daddy," I said, "Mr. Jim's badge turn up?"

Daddy's head was stuck down beside the engine. All I could

see was his rear end and his elbows. "Yeah, he found it hooked over the doorknob when he opened up this morning. Hand me that knucklebuster, will you?"

I fished it out of the toolbox and passed it to him. Daddy talked while he worked. "But it wasn't hanging there all by itself. There was a wing feather off some kind of bird, either a crow or a buzzard, and a little bit of something that looked like bone tied up in a black thread."

"What's it got all over it?"

"Wax," he said. "Somebody has gone and dripped black candle wax all over Bodine's name."

"It's Mr. Henry, sure as shootin'," I said, "he gone and put the root on Bodine. You gonna help him?"

"No," Daddy said.

"No Uncrossing Powder?"

"How you know about Uncrossing Powder?"

"You told me," I said.

"I did?"

"Yessir. Right after you went out to Mr. Henry's."

"Oh. I reckon I did. Take this wrench and hand me that belt."

"It's liable to kill him," I said.

Daddy took the belt and was quiet for a second or two. I could hear him breathing hard and grunting, trying to force it over the pulley and then said: "He don't think so."

"You know, don't you, Daddy?"

"Know what, son?"

Well, I said Bodine's name, but when I tried to say Bo

Manigault, I couldn't quite get it out. It was just like somebody had slapped me with a Shut Mouth Special. It ain't an easy thing, calling another man a murderer.

Sight or not, Daddy knew what I was thinking. He come up from under the hood all red in the face and with a broad stripe of grease across one cheek. He fixed me with those whupp-ass eyes and pointed his finger right in my face. "Don't you tell a living soul."

"Nossir," I said.

"Not Miss Marzette, neither. Nobody."

"But Miss Marzette hates him."

"That don't matter. You and I got trouble coming."

Damn, that would have knocked me right off a fence. My heart did a little flip-flop. "Me and you?" I asked.

"Not between you and me, boy, less you say one word about Bodine. But you and me together."

Well, that sounded a lot better. I couldn't have stood no trouble between us, but together, I reckoned we could have tackled most anything. I told him so and he give me a weak grin and held out the fan belt. "Get your skinny ass down to Billy Rhett's and get me a belt a half inch longer. I got to have this running before five."

And then he said, almost as an afterthought. "I got the results back from the state lab."

Chapter Sixteen

I tried, but we didn't make it by five. First off, it was a long way for a hog-cut boy. I know I was a lot better, years better, but I wasn't good enough. By the time I turned twenty I was about good enough to get drafted, but not quite. At fifty, I was gimping again and now I'm walking with this cane and I reckon if I live long enough I'll be on crutches and I'll have come full circle, like most of us generally do.

Don't think for a minute I'm complaining. Over the years, this tore up leg has served me pretty well. It kept me out of the Korean War and I never had to go to Berlin with Elvis and give the Russians the evil eye across that wall. Meantime, nobody expected me to play football or basketball and they always give me the deer stand easiest to get to, and damn near every girl I ever met set out to mother me, specially after I told them how I got cut up.

And I could always stand a little mothering. If I needed a little more, I would tell them about how Dr. Indigo stopped the blood, and talking a little light voodoo to a good looking gal is almost good as greasing her with Essence of Bend Over. A white gal, anyway. Mention root doctoring to one of our brown sisters and she'll leave you nothing but tracks and dust and sweet memories.

But anyway, I hobbled on down to Billy Rhett's and stood around waiting for the last-minute crowd to clear the counter. I stood there and waited and waved the belt and finally got his attention. I told him Daddy said it was a half inch too short and he grinned and said all us boys had the same problem and then he hollered up a Negro who disappeared into the back of the store and after what seemed a long while, come up with one an inch too long and said he hoped it would work.

It was pushing six o'clock by the time Daddy got the belt back on the car. It was as long as the other was short and it slipped and squealed when you stepped on the gas, but otherwise it worked OK.

Daddy and Bodine loaded up and damned if I wasn't going to go. Bodine or not, I climbed in the back seat and we headed on down Bay Street to Sea Island Rexall Drugs, the belt screeching like a Comanche.

Miss Marzette had already left by the time we got there. Daddy rattled the door til Squinchy come bustling up to let us in.

"Good afternoon, Sheriff. Bodine." He was kinda all itchy, you know like when you first get the chiggers. "What can I help you all with?"

Daddy looked him square in the eye. "Lead arsenate," he said.

Squinchy must have figured we was going to ask about his paregoric. He drew a blank, then his left eyelid started flapping like a shutter in a gale. "You all got rats?"

"We got at least one," Bodine said. "You sell lead arsenate?"

"Sure do, Deputy," he turned and headed for the pharmacy. "Come on back." Halfway there, he turned and held up his hand. It was trembling ever so slight. "Hold on, boys, I'll fetch it out." We stood there while he rummaged through some cabinets way out back in the part of the store hanging on pilings out over the Little Glory River. There was French windows facing the water, but you couldn't see through them, all boarded up from the blackout. I peeked around the corner, and there on a corner counter was a kerosene lamp with the chimney pulled off, some little bottle, and a smoked up old spoon.

Daddy seen it, too. But just like with Rauls selling likker after hours, Daddy didn't seem to care right then. I reckon he might have figured to get around to it someday, but he was back bird-dogging Dr. Indigo and he wasn't about to break point.

Squinchy come back with a quart can like what paint comes in, all bulging and rusty around the seams like something real nasty was trying to eat its way out. There was a yellowy label with skull and crossbones and words that read USP Paris Green.

Squinchy laid it on the counter and levered it open. Inside was something like that gaudy chartreuse mustard Japs eat on raw fish. "This here's the stuff, Sheriff. It'll kill damn near anything. You got potato beetles? Grasshoppers? Just dust a little of this around. You got a dog?"

"Nope," Daddy said.

"Good. Mix a spoon of this with peanut butter. Smear it on white bread and lay it out. It'll clean up your rats."

"Will it kill a man?" Bodine asked. It give me the willies to hear him talk about killing, but if it showed, nobody was paying me much attention. I was just a boy listening and remembering.

"Hell, yes!" Squinchy said. "If you get him to eat enough of it."

"What's enough?" Bodine asked.

"Damned if I know. I reckon it depends on the man. But a thimble full should do it."

"What would it do if it didn't kill him?" Daddy asked.

Squinchy got all twitchy again. "What's this about, Sheriff? Business or Official Business?"

"Look here, Elmore," Bodine said, "we asking the questions."

You could see Squinchy's adam's apple go up and down like a pump handle when it won't quite catch prime. He licked his lips, but there was no spit on his tongue. He was talking fast now. "Yessir, yessir, you asking the questions. I'm just curious, that's all. You all got yourself a nigger poisoning? I bet some gal dose her husband for dippin' his wick."

"No," Daddy said. "Not quite. What happens if you eat just a little of it?"

"It'll raise hell with you, I suppose. Here, let me check." He slapped the lid back on the can, went to the sink and washed up. "You can't be too careful with this stuff," he said over his shoulder. Then he flung his hands dry and reached above the counter and come up with a dusty little book and strung out words to put "Why Do the Heathen Rage?" to shame—*toxicology*, *anti-coagulant* and *cardiac arrhythmia*, and I don't know what all.

"Damnit, Elmore," Bodine said, "speak English."

"Cardiac," Daddy said. "That means heart. What's the rest of it?"

"Arrhythmia," Squinchy said. "You know, irregular."

"Murmurs?" Daddy asked.

"Murmurs," Squinchy said.

"You sell much of it?"

Squinchy paused and thought a few seconds. "Not so much any more. Back in the dry years when the locusts liked to et up everything, we sold it by the barrel."

"You keep track of it?"

"Sheriff, I keep track of everything." He gave a weak smile. "Just in case somebody needs to know."

"Well," Daddy said, "I need to know."

Elmore reached back beneath the counter and hauled out a ledger about half as big as a good-sized stingeree. He flopped it open and went to the last page, then worked his way forward, running his finger up the handwritten columns. "Humm, let's see here. Lydia Pinkham, morphine, codeine," he squinted at the page, "para....well, there's nothing serious here."

Bodine looked over his shoulder and they flipped the page and kept on going. Finally, Bodine sang out, "Whoa, what's this?"

Daddy jumped into the huddle and Squinchy looked like he was about to break out with St. Vitus dance. "Henry Manigault," Bodine read, sounding out the syllables like a third grader. "Paris Green February fourth, nineteen and forty-five." He flipped another page. "Henry Manigault, Paris Green, December One, nineteen and forty-four. Hot damn, Mac, you got him now!"

Daddy just stood there dumbfounded, like he had been slapped up side the head with a two-by-four. I could see a vein on his neck, blip, blip, working with his pulse. I slid over and looked at the page. In each entry, right next to Mr. Henry's name, was the clerk who had made the sale.

Marzette Goodwine.

Chapter Seventeen

Nearly three years to the day after Harley Davidson and I sat beneath the statue of Wade Hampton waiting on the trial of a Williman Island bootlegger, we was back there again, waiting on the trial of the world's greatest root doctor. You can call that progress if you want. I don't know what to call it.

In the meantime, that damn Hitler had just about give up and would soon shoot himself rather than surrender, but the Japs was still hanging on and me and Harley was keeping up with our air raid and blackout work, just in case the Japs slipped one over on us like they did at Pearl Harbor. Will Mahoney's headlines were getting better and better; not necessarily more creative, mind you, but they was better news: "Krauts Freeze Up in Russia," "Marines Take Iwo Jima," and finally, "Ike Giving Japs Hell in Pacific." When somebody pointed out that General Dwight David Eisenhower was in Europe at the time, old Will Mahoney took another drink and waved his hand and said, "Hell, they know what I mean!"

We might have just about won the war, but Daddy and I had one going of our own, one we could not win. And my insides was feeling like they was full of busted glass.

"Get your ass upstairs," Daddy said, "and get on that home-work." We were out in the yard, fresh from finding Miss Marzette had been selling Dr. Indigo lead arsenate. She was standing on the stoop, hair up in a kerchief and the rest of her in an apron, smiling like she did ever-time we got home. But she took one look at Daddy and she must have known some-thing was up.

I couldn't look her in the eye. "Evening, Miss Marzette," I said as I brushed on by. I tried to grab her hand and squeeze it to let her know that I loved her anyway. I made a snatch at it but missed.

Daddy just stood and looked at her and waited til he heard my feet on the stairs. I slipped across my bedroom and eased open the sash, the one facing north right above the stoop roof. They were already into it by the time I got my head out the window.

Daddy was talking. "...and you have aided and abetted a felony. Henry Manigault was practicing medicine without a license. He recklessly endangered the lives of two dozen boys. I'll have to question you, maybe even arrest you. You might have to testify. And there might be federal charges. Assisting in the Avoidance of Induction, that's Federal, Marzette! And Conspiracy? Jesus Christ, they are going to put your ass under the jail!"

Miss Marzette fired right back, her voice all crackling with rage. "It would please me, Mac McCloud, if you did not refer to my posterior with such familiarity! And you know better than to take the Savior's name in vain!"

"In vain?" Daddy hollered, "In vain? You damn right it's in vain! I call out Jesus God Why and He don't say a thing! This whole shitaree is in vain! You, me, everything! You know I been working on this case! Why in the hell didn't you tell me?"

"You drag me before a judge! I'll tell him what I'll tell you now! I sold Mr. Henry poison for the rats in his chicken coop! And then I'll never speak to you again."

There was a long silence, then Daddy's voice got all sad and low. "Why Marzette? Why?"

"You know why, Mac. Some things might be legal, but that don't make 'em right. Some things ain't legal, but that don't make 'em wrong."

"But I'm a lawman, Marzette, I can't make that call."

"Oh, you can, Mac, and you do. That same ledger will tell you how much paregoric comes in and how little gets sold. There ought to be cases back there, but there ain't. But you don't care about that, do you? Rauls is selling whiskey, but you won't arrest him 'cause you need your little spy to watch after Dr. Indigo."

"How you know about Samuel Dibble?"

"I know everything, Mac."

They quit talking for a minute and I was about to bust to know what they was doing. But hanging out the window like that, I couldn't see a thing. "Kiss her, Daddy, kiss her," I was saying to myself. "Put your arms around her and snatch off that kerchief and put your nose in that red hair and smell that sweat she got from cleaning our house. Remember what you all did when you ran off down the rice dike road right after you got back from the pony patrol. Tell her how much you love her and how much I do, too. Come on, Daddy, come on. The hell with them Square Head Germans and the Flat Face Japs. We 'bout whipped them, anyway. Get off your high horse Malcolm Edward McCloud the Sixth. There's flesh and blood and bone right there in front of you. She loves us, Daddy. Don't let her get away. Kiss her, Daddy, kiss her!"

But then Daddy said, "Then you know Mr. Henry wasn't killing no rats."

Lordy, where is a Shut Mouth Special when you need it? I was so damn mad at him I wanted to kick a hole in the plaster wall and stomp and beller, but I dasn't since they would have just moved out into the yard and kept it up and Daddy for sure would have whupped me later on for listening in.

"Maybe I did and maybe I didn't. Do I need a lawyer to keep talking to you?" Her blood was up again.

"You might think about getting you one," Daddy said.

"On my wages? I'll just sit in jail, a prisoner of The Lord!"

"Maybe you could get your damn Mr. Henry to put the root on me!"

Miss Marzette let that one slide and changed tack. "Maybe Indigo saved those boys just like he saved yours. You ever think of that?"

"Hell, yes, I think about it!"

"Don't you swear at me!"

"I wasn't swearing at you!"

"Well, quit swearing altogether. Mac, you're sending them

out in buses and they're coming back in boxes. You won't let most of them even vote! It ain't their war and it just ain't right."

Well, I could have guessed what was coming next. Daddy might have loved our glory of Negroes, and the great gumbo that come about from us mixing up Injuns and Scots and English and Africans here on these sunny islands. But he was real weak on social activism. The do-gooders were generally from up north and all of us have had a belly full of Yankees ever since General Sherman got so handy with his matches. Daddy believed you ought to tackle it one man at a time. Meet him in the middle of the road. Cut him some slack. Love your neighbors, black or white. But keep it private. I seen the day when he was proud to give Harley Davidson money for college, though it didn't do no good, and years later, cut a check that helped Harley's daughter, Miss Evangeline, bust into an all-white girls' school. But if Will Mahoney would have gotten ahold of it, Daddy would have just curled up and died.

And if you wanted to spin him up real quick, just slightly suggest that the Sheriff of Calhoun County should somehow be responsible for what was wrong and for setting things right. "Well, Miz Roosevelt," he said, the words fairly dripping with sarcasm, "you're about two hundred years behind schedule. By the time you get caught up, we'll all be speaking Japanese."

Lordy, it pained me to hear it but I did. And then I heard something that pained me more. The clack, clack, clack of her heels on the front steps and the swish and sigh of the screen door and Daddy's lonesome shoes on the hall flooring. And then she was gone, gone, and I was heartbroke and miserable.

I don't even want to tell you about the supper that went to waste that night, or the one I didn't eat the night after and the breakfast I picked at in between and how after a few days I got like somebody had put the root on me. I had to eat or else I would have took to bed and who knows if I would have ever got back up. Even Miss Althea moped around like her dog had got run over.

Miss Marzette was everywhere I looked, everyplace I was, in the garden, in the kitchen, dusting up the hall, in the cab of Daddy's old truck, and way out in the oleander hedges where we had corralled those lightning bugs for that Injun lamp, picking me up from school, tucking me in and pulling the sheets up around my ears like only she could do it, behind my eyelids, in my dreams, and under my skin. It was just like somebody you loved had up and died, nearly as bad as quitting smoking.

Daddy ate and walked and worked like he always did, but you could tell he just didn't have no conviction, dragging himself through his days like he had ten pounds of lead in each shoe. He had to go out and arrest Dr. Indigo. God knows what that must have been like. Maybe he was so mad at Miss Marzette, it was easy for him. But I doubt it. Maybe they each put on their blue glasses and looked at each other a long time and maybe each of them said this is what I got to do, this is what you got to do. I just don't know. I wish I could tell you all of it, and I sometimes think I should make up what I don't know just to pull the pieces all together. But I promised I'd tell you only what I know to be true, so I will.

So, Daddy arrested him and Bodine locked him up. They

hauled Mr. Henry to court and the judge set bail at ten thousand dollars and Mr. Henry went back to his cell and everybody figured he'd be there awhile. I was primed for slipping down to see him, to thank him again for saving my life and telling him I was sorry and if there was anything I could do, short of busting him out, I would do it.

But I would have had to dodge both Daddy and Bodine and I never got the chance. The next morning one of Rauls' cabbies showed up with Miss Marzette in the back seat and a beat up old foot locker hanging out the trunk. The cabbie wrestled it into the office and Miss Marzette breezed in like the Queen of Sheba and opened it and hauled out the wrinkled singles and fives and threw them on Daddy's desk til there was a pile you couldn't hardly shake hands across. Daddy counted it twice and Bodine three times and they couldn't argue with the arithmetic, so they turned Mr. Henry loose and Miss Marzette took him home.

I wish I could tell you how that all came about, too. How he got word to Miss Marzette to bring the trunk and bail him out. But I can't, so I won't.

Everybody wondered what the doctor would do. Would he root the court like he had done before, chew a High John the Conqueror and send the judge rushing off to spend two days on the commode? Would the bailiff clutch his throat and gasp and keel over? Would the solicitor wobble and stagger and fall? Would lightning strike, the power go off, or the fountain run red with blood like it did in "Why Do the Heathen Rage?" We was wondering, too, me and Harley Davidson, beneath that statue of Wade Hampton, when we heard the stirring and shuffling through the high open windows and we knew it was time to go in.

Chapter Eighteen

But Mr. Henry Manigault, the great Dr. Indigo, fooled us again. He didn't root the whole damn county when his boy turned up dead. And he didn't do it now. He had him Robert Barnwell Sams, a slick white lawyer from Charleston with a Broad Street address—what Daddy called "Shark Alley," where you fairly trip over barristers and real estate men.

Daddy figured it was a open and shut case. They had a suspect and the juice. They had the ledger. They had the state crime lab report. Sure, they needed a witness, but a witness was hard to come by. Daddy knew better than to call Miss Marzette. They had Squinchy lined up, but he couldn't say much and you couldn't have beat testimony out of a Negro with a billy-stick. But this was 1945 in South Carolina District Court, and four out of five would get you hard time, every time.

Mr. Henry was old and skinny and frail, and I reckon if they put him in jail for even a month, he might have never made it back out. But he didn't look too worried. He sat there at the defendant's table, the mourner's bench as Daddy called it, in a suit like you'd pick out for a funeral, no cane, no blue glasses, looking about as harmless as a preacher in the Second Sanctified Brethren. He give me a nod and I give him a little smile and I went and found me a seat on the front row, way off to the left where they penned the Yankee mules, where the floor is tore up and the seats real close to the bench, where I wouldn't miss a thing.

The place was packed, as you might imagine, Negroes on one side, whites on the other. The sentiments were pretty well divided, too, Negroes wanting him a-turned loose, and whites 'bout ready to string him up since they figured he didn't love his country.

It's damn funny how that works. Get you a war going and beat the drum and nobody almost never raises hell and asks why, and they don't never get after the government and keel haul them about why they let things get so bad they was nothing left to do but fight. They haul five million men across two oceans, and come up short a million when they haul them back. They could fill New York City with the widows and orphans they made, but they won't make cars and refrigerators. They quit selling tires and gas and if you didn't get a garden in the ground you wouldn't be too well fed. They plow up half the world and bomb hell out of the other and Jesus weeps while the chaplains go out and bless the whole damn thing and people stand in line to die.

And they figured Mr. Henry didn't love his country? Hell, he loved this ground and he loved this water and he loved his people, and he gone and put his fanny on the line for them. I reckon that's country enough for most anybody.

But back then I hadn't quite figured all that out, and I was all tore up about it. Here was Daddy, trying to run up the man who saved me. Here was Miss Marzette, run off because of it. Here was Lil Mac, just a-itching to stand up and holler "Hey, this man saved me when I was hog-cut and fixing to die!" But I wouldn't 'cause I couldn't and I was just dying inside.

Well, the bailiff sung out and the judge come in and set down and took a passing swipe with his gavel and the solicitor got up and read the charge.

"Your honor, today we have the State of South Carolina vs. Henry Manigault, alias Dr. Indigo...."

That sent Robert Barnwell Sams to his feet, his nose beet red and his jowls a flopping. "Objection!" he hollered. He was one of those bilious old Charleston lawyers who can argue water into running uphill. He was big as an oil drum, with a voice like he just gargled with castor oil.

The judge give him the fish eye. "Counselor, what in the world is wrong with you? This is no time for an objection. This trial has not even begun. What possibly could you find in the charge that's objectional?"

"Your honor, my client, Mr. Henry Manigault, has been charged with practicing medicine without a license...."

Now it was the solicitor's turn to interrupt. "Which was just what I was going to say...."

The judge shut him down. "Let Mr. Sams finish, please."

"Thank you, your honor. As I was going to say, my client has been charged with practicing medicine without a license.

He is not being charged with being Dr. Indigo. The state has no proof that he is Dr. Indigo, or that such a person even exists."

"Your honor," the solicitor said, "the state intends to show that Henry Manigault and Dr. Indigo are one in the same. And that is crucial to the successful prosecution of this case."

Well, the judge was stumped. "Approach the bench," he said.

Well, they went into their little huddle, the judge leaning over and them two old blisters on their tip-toes. They was all so worked up, they forgot to whisper. And I heard nearly every damn word.

"Boys," the judge said, "we can't keep this up. Hell, we'll be here all day!"

"Look here, Judge," Sams said, "if you let him call that old nigger Dr. Indigo, it's a clear presumption of guilt."

The solicitor fired back. "Hell, he is guilty! What do it matter what we call him? Judge, this country's at war. We make this stick and the Feds will be all over him."

"Judge, you let that statement stand, and I'll appeal."

Both of them looked at Sams like he had just broke out in Hebrew. "Sammy, you won't do that!" the solicitor said.

"Yes, I will!"

"Why?"

"'Cause he pays me."

"Pays you? This ain't pro-boner?"

"What?"

"Pro-boner, you know, free?"

"Hell, I don't work for free, specially for a nigger." He nodded towards the solicitor, got all syrupy. "You know, my colleague is right. We got us a war going. I got stamps, but I can't get tires. I got chits, but I can't get gas. This nigger's got money!"

"That's 'cause he's Dr. Indigo!"

Well, they kept at it, jawing the law and the war, and maybe fishing and women, too, and pretty soon the judge had enough of it and said something I didn't catch. Then the solicitor walked back to his side of the court and stood there kind of hopeless and Robert Barnwell Sams went to his a-grinning like a possum.

And then the judge give both of them the evil eye and asked if they was ready to proceed. They nodded and the solicitor read the charges again: "The State of South Carolina vs. Henry Manigault..." he paused and rolled his eyes, "...for practicing medicine without a license."

That brought a stir out of the crowd, some amening amongst the Negroes and a general cussing from the whites. The judge gaveled them down and the solicitor went on.

"The state contends this is a simple case. The defendant, Henry Manigault, on at least two occasions purchased lead arsenate from Sea Island Rexall Drugs. Now we all know that arsenic is a deadly poison. But in small doses, and we will offer expert testimony to this effect, it will cause cardiac arrhythmia, the hippity-hoppity heart. After an entire busload of draftees, twenty-four in number, failed their induction physicals, Sheriff Mac McCloud apprehended one of those individuals and recovered this sample."

He pulled the half pint flask from his briefcase and swirled it around over his head. There was an inch of milky green liquid in the bottom, like lemonade gone sour in the sun. It didn't look like anything you'd want to drink, war or no. He handed it to the judge. "I'll ask this to be accepted as the state's Exhibit A."

He strutted around, real proud of himself. "We intend to show that Henry Maginault mixed this lead arsenate with moonshine whiskey and sold it to a number of Negro draftees."

Well, I was feeling real sorry for Mr. Henry right then, but it only got worse. That's the way it goes, you'll find if you ever go to court. The prosecutor reads the riot act and you figure they just ain't no hope til the defense kicks into gear. They read the lab report. They hauled out the ledger, and then Squinchy. Daddy took the stand and told how he had shook that boy til he come up with the flask. Of course, he didn't say it just like that, but everybody got the drift anyway.

And then it was Robert Barnwell Sams' turn. He come up from his chair, all puffed up like a turkey gobbler, face about seven shades of red and purple. But before he could flap, the judge looked at his watch. "Mr. Sams," he said, "the court is getting hungry. The court finds it twenty minutes past dinnertime." Then the gavel came down. "Court's in recess til 2:30 this afternoon."

Well, we all filed out. Everybody but me and Daddy and Mr. Henry and Harley Davidson. Mr. Henry looked at Daddy and Daddy looked at him and Mr. Henry smiled this gatory sort of smile and reached into his pocket and pulled out his blue glasses and Harley Davidson figured he'd wait for us outside. Mr. Henry put those glasses on and Daddy put his on, too, and the air was just a crackling and I was about to jump right out of my skin.

"You remember what I told you, Mac McCloud," Mr. Henry said in his deep sad voice. "That day on the beach. You take care of my people."

"You remember what I said," Daddy come back, slow, too, but deliberate, "I'm going to take care of all the people."

"I told you, white people don't need no looking after. They help they selves."

"No, Mr. Henry, we need looking after, too." He paused a second, or three. "And thanks once more for saving this boy."

Mr. Henry looked at me and smiled again. "Yessir, I believe he was worth savin'. He gone have a story to tell some day."

Well, I didn't know quite what to make of that. There weren't much need of me telling stories so long as Daddy was around. And I didn't figure any of this was special. Even with the war and the conjuring and me getting my leg tore up and all the misery over Miss Marzette, it was just what life was like, so far as I could tell, common as the full moon high tide. Back then, I just didn't know no better.

"Yeah," Daddy said, "if we can keep them hogs from eatin' him."

"That boy gone eat a lot of hogs," Mr. Henry said, "but ain't none gone eat him."

Well, I was about ready for some good news. And I was hoping Robert Barnwell Sams would come up with at least one dead rat and a lab report that said he had arsenic in him.

As it turned out, it really didn't matter. Mr. Henry turned and walked out and Daddy followed and I looked over at the judge's bench and, great-God-a-mighty-damn, that bottle of hippity-hoppity heart juice was gone.

Chapter Nineteen

Come two-thirty, the lawyers and the bailiff and the judge filed back in and they all seen it was gone and for about a hour and a half, that courthouse was a hornet nest. They looked high and low, under all the benches, in the judge's chambers, in the bathrooms, colored and white, and in the oleander bushes below the windows. Bodine stood all the Negroes along the west wall, right under that picture of Moses handing down the Ten Commandments, and he and the bailiff patted them down. They got a couple of straight razors, a dozen plugs of tobacco, half a marijuana cigarette and upwards of a thousand lies. But they got no hippity-hoppity heart juice. Robert Barnwell Sams was quick to remind everybody that no evidence was no case. So Henry Manigault, old Dr. Indigo, went home. His days was short, but they was free.

Right away, they figured I done it. If Daddy hadn't been there, I reckon that bailiff would have shook me like Daddy shook that boy outside the Swing Low Sweet Juke Joint. But he could a-shook til my eyes rolled round backwards and my fillings fell out and it wouldn't have done him no good.

We say this prayer at Church of the Cross, where everybody kneels and tucks their heads way down low and gets real solemn, even if they don't really mean it. They say something like "Forgive us for what we have done, and for what we have left undone." Most folks worry over the first half, the likker they drunk and the loving they snuck and the neighbors they treated poorly. But the second half really sets Jesus to weeping.

Sure, the first snagged me. But if I was fool enough for the first, I should have been brave enough for the second. And I'd give you a fifty dollar cast net to be able to say I took it. But I told you from the first I'd tell you only the truth.

First, there was Daddy and Mr. Henry standing there talking and staring and damn near giving me the hippity-hoppity heart. I seen the flask one minute and the next minute I didn't.

Mr. Henry might have palmed it, but Daddy would have seen him, less he was slicker than a Savannah pickpocket, where they come floating up behind you with hands like butterflies.

Maybe Mr. Henry conjured it clean away, like the Negroes said. You can believe that if you want.

Daddy told me once, when you set out to solve a crime, you look for opportunity and motive. And he was long on both, and given the judicial standards of the day, there could have been a case made against him. But nobody was about to accuse the Sheriff of Calhoun County, least of all, me.

Daddy told me a lot over the years, swindles and gambling and moonshining and whoring and car wrecks and cuttings and shootings and mysterious deaths, but the secret of what really happened to that hippity-hoppity juice he took to his grave.

Wherever it went, Daddy wasn't about to give up trying to get Dr. Indigo. Maybe he wasn't really out to get him, but just checking up on him in a friendly sort of way.

Sure, Dr. Indigo saved my life and maybe Daddy saved his. But it was a one-time deal. If Daddy didn't find no more hippi-ty-hoppity juice floating around and the Army didn't turn up no more busloads of heart murmurs, it'd be right as rain. But any more foolishness, and Daddy would have had to go after him again.

So Daddy kept Samuel Dibble in likker money through most of June of 1945, very privately, of course, so Miss Marzette wouldn't get wind of it.

Yes, she was back. Sweet Jesus, what a glorious day, four days after the trial, Rauls' cabbie dropping her off at the front stoop, in one of those trim little suits women wore in those days. It looked more like a uniform than what a woman ought to wear, and she had on high heel shoes and stockings like cop-per screen wire with the seams down the back. But that didn't matter. She was better looking than ever.

Daddy was working late and I was fresh home from school and she took me into the parlor and we pulled up a couple of chairs and she held my hand across Grandma Heyward's little table.

"I'm sorry, Lil Mac," she said, all brimming and sniffling and smelling like peaches, "for leaving you that-a-way."

They say you learn about women from your momma. I never had a momma long enough to remember, but I had Miss Marzette and I was learning fast. Way down inside, I hated

Daddy for running her off. I hated her for leaving. I hated myself for hating the both of them, and most of all for being so damn lonesome. I was all bound up in a cold black blanket and I couldn't have cut my way loose with a switchblade knife.

But in fourteen seconds I was ready to crawl, ready to say I was sorry for ever-thing I never done. Ready to say, "Hell, yes, it was all my own damn fault for damn near getting killed by that boar pig, for getting out of the truck in the first place. My fault for thinking I could turn that big bastard with my pellet gun. My fault for getting saved by Dr. Indigo and for Hitler and Tojo, too!" And then I would have throwed living and breathing in for good measure.

But I didn't. "That's OK, Miss Marzette," I said.

She squeezed my hand and her tears were a-catching, and she all kind of ran together, red hair and green eyes and that little ski-jump nose in a confusion of ever woman-thing God can throw at you. About the time I couldn't hardly stand it no more, she said. "I been speaking to Mr. Henry about it. He says you're a good boy but might turn sour if you don't get a momma. He says your daddy is a good man who would be a lot better if he had him a woman. He says the Lord is working even when you think He ain't. I know I done you wrong, Lil Mac, but I'm taking my comfort in what Mr. Henry said."

"Yassum," I said. And I could have kissed ever one of those freckles.

But I left that for Daddy. He come home about quarter after nine and when he seen her washing up the dinner dishes, he stood there in the door with his funny little half smile, dumbstruck, like he had been slapped with a Shut Mouth Special. Miss Marzette had to ease him to the kitchen table and set him down. She brought his dinner from the oven and sat down across from him and he forked off a piece of pork chop and looked at it, then at her, and just sat there, holding that piece of meat til it got cold.

"Mac, honey," she said, "ain't you going to eat your supper?"

"What?" he said.

I had et already, so I turned in and left them to themselves.

But I got to tell you about Sam Dibble and Bodine. It was one of those late July days when the heat and the lazy light sets the cicadas to yammering, when the air is thick as corn syrup and the tide runs sort of listless and slow and even the pelicans can't flap with much conviction.

I was helping Daddy paw through the mail when Sam Dibble come sliding in the door, all beaded up and greasy from the sun beating on the roof of that taxi. "Yessir, Mr. Mac," he said, "the doctor still workin'."

I had graduated from topping off the oil and airing up the tires. Bodine couldn't hardly read and Daddy would tie right into a sea story or a windy hunting tale, but the sea of paper that come to him every day was enough to swamp him. Sure, he kept his eye on the *Hound Dog Report,* and tried to fill out paperwork for the solicitor, but the bills from Lonnie Mulligan and Billy Rhett, and for the chicken necks and rice and bologna and white bread for the jail, and all the letters from the legally aggrieved and politically afflicted would stomp him right down.

So I pitched in. I'd open it all and stuff the envelopes in the trash and lay what was left on his desk. And I'd tell him what they said and he'd tell me where to file them away. I don't know if all the business got took care of, but at least you could see the top of his desk.

"What you got, Sam?"

"They still comin', a solid stream of um." His throat was working and he held his little cabbie hat in his hands and wrung it like a dishrag. "Womens and mens, but there's a peculiar thing, Mr. Mac."

Daddy put down the *Hound Dog Report.* "What's that, Sam?"

"Them boy."

"What boys?"

"You know, all them young boy. Ever-body else they breeze right in. But he won't let them young boy shrew the do'."

"He don't?"

"Naw, suh. He meet um on the porch, run um off. They holler and moan and go way wif long face."

"Huh," Daddy said.

"He say he gone hep um, but he don' hep um."

"You sure?"

"Well suh, he ain' do nothin' I see. But you know the doctor."

Daddy grinned and grabbed his wallet. "Thanks, Sam. That's the best news you brung me yet."

"Twenty dollar? Great Gawd, Mr. Mac! I sho buss um loose this time!"

"Don't you go drinking that all up in one night, you hear."

Sam grinned til you'd-a thought his face would-a split clean in two. "Naw suh. I stretch this drunk out all week."

So the doctor was working with spirits and not potions. There weren't no laws against hexing, even if you put somebody in the ground. But you couldn't practice medicine without a license. Daddy was real pleased with himself. And it was only going to get better.

I was fanning through the rest of the mail when I come up with a government letter for James L. Bodine. I puzzled over it for a half minute.

"What you got, Bub?" Daddy asked.

"Durned if I know." I was pushing thirteen, but I still wouldn't cuss around Daddy. "It's for Mr. Jim."

"Lemme see it."

I passed it over. Daddy looked at it. "Here, Jim, something for you."

Bodine snatched it up. "What the hell?"

He tore it open and fairly bellered. "Greeting? Hell, they can't do this! The war's most over! And I'm too damned old!" He huffed and blubbered and went down the lines. "Report at four-thirty on July 30? Jesus Christ, you got to help me Mac!"

Daddy smiled like Dr. Indigo did that day in court. And then he reached into his shirt pocket and hauled out those blue glasses.

"Mac?" Bodine said. "Mac?"

Well, Bodine should have called out for Jesus, 'cause calling for Daddy didn't do him no good at all. He showed up when they told him to and Daddy made sure he got on that bus and the bus rattled on off towards Columbia, hauling the oldest draftee in the history of the Second World War. And I was the happiest kid in Calhoun County, South Carolina.

Chapter Twenty

About two weeks later, Daddy come home with a headline that read "Crazed Jap Suicide Run." I put down my homework, fetched up Harley Davidson and read him the particulars. They would take a Jap and preach a funeral over him. They would teach him to take off but not to land. They would give him enough gas to get there but not back. They would give him a bomb and a shot of likker and cut him loose. The Navy was catching hell, seven ships sunk and twenty more hit and men floundering in the water and getting et up by sharks.

The *Palmetto Post* was pretty well et up, too, all faded out and spotted up with the horseflies Daddy swatted off the squad car windshield. If we'd have read the date, we'd a known it was six months old. But we didn't and we got war fever all over again.

We had got a little slack on our air raid and blackout work. The Square Head Germans had give up and, besides, way up in that oak tree, the skeeters liked to ate us alive. But that paper fired us up and, skeeters or no, we figured to give her another few nights, just in case.

I had taken to driving the pickup—not down the highway, you understand, but just around the plantation. I was pretty good at it, but had trouble with the gears, so Daddy would put it in second and I would always park where I didn't have to back up. I had to smoke the clutch to get her rolling, and, at twenty, the engine was about to crawl out from under the hood, but it sure beat walking, specially with my bum leg.

Miss Althea made us up a couple of ham sandwiches and drew us a Mason jar of ice tea. I put on my Official Junior Blackout Compliance Warden armband and dug out my little book about ships and loose lips just in case we ran across anybody to read it to. And then we loaded up and drove down to the big oak with the lookout we made from the siding off the back of the old chicken coop.

It was glorious up there in the crown of that tree, the river coiled and shining like bright steel, the patchwork rice fields stretching off toward the southwest and the great dark wall of tupeloes and cypress beyond. There was a sad old moon and a few pinprick stars a-glimmering and a-winking way overhead like they was saying, "You all go ahead with what you're doin', all your lying and thieving and your killin' and conjurin' 'cause it just don't make much difference to us."

Them stars have seen it all, and they'll see more yet before Jesus comes back. Sometimes at night when it drizzles, I lay up in bed and think it might have got to some of them and they're weeping just like Jesus. And when one of them finally gets where he can't stand no more, he jumps off the great black dome of the sky and comes flaming down in a streak of light and you'd think it's pretty if you don't think it was a star killing himself.

But right then we was thinking about Japs and not Jesus, not stars.

Pretty soon, we was thinking about skeeters.

You'd think the bugs round here was unionized Democrat. They team up and split the time, so making us miserable won't be too hard on any one shift. We got black skeeters the size of dimes hatching out in the woods springtimes, pea-sized convict striped devils in midsummer, and, when the swamps dry up in August, the little brown bastards that hatch out in rice fields descend upon us.

But that ain't the end of it. The skeeters can only do so much. They pester you early mornings and late evenings, and the gnats take up the slack in between. There's deerflies when you move in the sun and horseflies when you sit in the shade and ticks all the time and chiggers that can gnaw on your nubbins bad enough to send you to the 'mergency room.

It took about five minutes for the skeeters to find us. You wouldn't think something so small could hurt so bad. Me and Harley swatted and scratched and cussed and finally we was about to give her up and climb down and go to bed.

"Look here, Mr. Lil Mac," Harley said, "we got to do something 'bout these bugs. Didn't they give you no dope in that blackout warden kit?"

"No," I said, "they ain't give us shit."

"Well, what was they thinkin', anyway? They must have knowed we'd be working in the dark."

"Damned if I know. Maybe they needed it somewheres else."

"Well, we shore need it here. What we gone to do?" He rattled a finger in his left ear. "I can't stand much more of this."

"Let's make us a smudge," I said.

"A smudge?"

"Yeah, man, bust up some of them cedar boughs and get her going."

Harley took a swipe at the side of his face. "Damn, Mr. Lil Mac, you shore come up with some good ones." He was halfway down the ladder when he hollered up at me. "How is we gone have us a fire way up in this tree?"

Well, I was stumped for a minute, but then it come to me. "Pull one of them hubcaps off the truck. Use that big old screwdriver under the seat."

I could hear him stumbling around in the dark, the swish and snap of cedar branches, the *k-wang* of a hubcap coming off the pickup wheel, and finally the creak of the ladder under his weight.

He shoved the hubcap and the boughs up onto the platform, then clumb up behind them. I wadded up the cedar and tore the back page from the blackout book, the one where you were supposed to write down all the violations. There weren't a damn thing on it so I figured it wouldn't hurt to put it to good use. I cupped the match and held it low just in case there was any crazed Jap suiciders hanging around and, pretty soon, the thick white smoke was a-rolling out of our official observation post like when Willie Simmons lit a hickory fire in that old phone booth.

But damn, that cedar smoke was most bad as the skeeters. A smudge is good on the ground, where you can stand in it and get it on your skin and in your clothes and in your hair. Up there in that live oak, we done that quick enough. But then, there was no getting away from it. You may think it smells good when you pull blankets out of a cedar chest, or when you nose a dog that's been laying up in a pile of shavings. But just you try breathing it steady and you'll change your mind in a hurry. We leaned this way and that, but it followed us which ever way we went.

'Bout the time we was about to bail out, Harley Davidson grabbed my shoulder and pointed off to the southeast. "Damn, Mr. Lil Mac, look at that!"

I hung upwind as best I could, wiped my nose, and squinted the water out of my eyes. Way down along the riverbank, way off beyond Albemarle, where the Little Glory cuts east on its last run to the sea, there was this dull glow deep down in the bushes, a bright fan of light up into the trees beyond.

"Hot damn, Mr. Lil Mac," Harley said, "we got us a violation."

I snatched up the book. "Where's the pencil?"

Harley Davidson patted his pockets. "You got one?"

"Hell, no! I thought you did."

The wind caught the cedar smoke and coiled it around his head like a wreath. "We got to do something, Mr. Lil Mac! Them Japs might make a dive on us!"

I swung down onto the ladder. "Come on, Harley, let's check it out!"

He come down the ladder behind me. "Hell, Mr. Lil Mac, that's five mile away!"

"We'll take the truck!"

The starter clicked and whirred and the engine sneezed and caught. I worked the footfeed and eased out the clutch and it slipped and smoked til the cab smelt like burnt rags. The tires spun in the sand, then caught in the grass and the truck lurched forward til me and Harley's heads bounced off the back glass, and all the junk Daddy kept up on the dashboard, all the nails and bolts and shotgun shells and papers and I don't know what-all, come a-showering down on us.

But we was moving, really moving. Up the riverbank, cross the pasture where the cows blinked and stared like they couldn't believe what we was doing, past the big house, all dark now at midnight, down the driveway and right on the blacktop rocking down through the swamps toward Albemarle, the engine howling like a banshee. "Great God, Mr. Lil Mac, yo daddy gone tan our hides!"

"This is war," I said. "We all got to do what we can!"

We squalled around the corner onto Bay Street, shuttered and forelorn, roared past Squinchy's store where Miss Marzette caused all that trouble. We hooked a right onto the bridge, and way up under the draw we seen the light again, no more than a mile away, a long yellow tongue licking up the dark. "Hell," Harley Davidson said, "it ain't nothin' but a house afire."

"How you talk, Harley? There ain't no houses down there!"

"You right. Wonder what the hell it is?"

"Damned if I know. But we gonna make 'em put it out."

"Yessir. You got that book to read 'em?"

"Oh, shit, I left it in the tree!"

"Let's go back an' fetch 'um."

"No time for that. I can remember most of what it says."

We kept on going, way down past Blocker's store where the mournful oaks closed in and we couldn't see the light no more, then further where the sky opened up past those big old tomato fields and there the light was again, just begging the crazed Jap suiciders to bomb hell out of us.

We took a right on that little sandy track that runs down towards Barrel Landing and then right again and the road played out in a tangle of wax myrtle and cassena and we couldn't go no more. I hit the key and we coasted to a stop the way Daddy did outside the Swing Low Sweet Juke Joint. The engine sighed and gurgled and then went tick, tick, tick, the way engines do when you shut them down. And then there was nothing to do but walk.

We was a hundred feet from the fire when I heard a voice. It warn't English and my blood run cold.

"Japs," Harley whispered. "They done slipped one over on us." He turned back toward the truck. "Come on, Mr. Lil Mac, let's get the hell out of here!"

I grabbed his elbow to keep him from bolting. We whispered back and forth. "Uh-uh, Harley, we got to do our duty."

"Mr. Lil Mac, I 'bout to dooty my britches right now."

"They must have put men ashore to light a fire to guide the planes."

"You reckon?"

"Shore. What else would they be up to? Come on, let's crawl."

"Crawl? You loss you mine? You get us snakebit for shore."

Well, he was right about that. There's some powerful snakey woods here in Calhoun County, all loaded up with copperheads and rattlers and moccasins. They lay low during the day, and come out and crawl around at night, just like the spirits. But if they was Japs out there, I just had to know it. I eased down on my belly and gatored toward the light.

"Wait up, Mr. Lil Mac, you ain't leaving me here in the dark."

So we slithered along, closer and closer, me first, Harley next, his head never more than six inches from my foot. The jabbering kept up in some kind of tune, but not like no music I ever heard.

Harley Davidson seen it first. He grabbed my leg and whispered, "Oh Lordy, Mr. Lil Mac!"

There on the bank of the river was a driftwood fire. And there by the fire was old Dr. Indigo.

Sometimes I call him Dr. Indigo and sometimes Mr. Henry and sometimes it gets kinda mixed up in my mind. But that night on the bank of the Little Glory, there weren't no Mr. Henry around. Sure, he had on his Mr. Henry courtroom suit. But this time he had his glasses and cane and he was speaking in unknown tongues, and taking up some shuffling kind of dance, heel and toe, heel and toe, like the old ring shout in the Negro churches. The flames was rising, falling, shimmering in the sea breeze, throwing crawly shadows across his face, across the sand, on the trees beyond. When he turned his head, the fire slapped behind those glasses, and I seen the whites of his eyes as he danced.

I heard a rustle behind me and reached around and snagged Harley Davidson before he could high tail it. I got him by the leg and he whipped around like a gator to tear my hand loose but then I got him in a hammer lock and I had him. We rolled and thrashed in the saw palmettoes til a deef man could have heard us and a blind man could have seen us. But when Dr. Indigo come round again, he passed us by, thank God, his eyes fixed off somewheres in middle distance.

Dr. Indigo held his cane in his left hand and pumped it with the rhythm of his feet. And then he hauled something from his pocket, held it over his head, and tossed it to the flames.

It looked like some kind of mojo to me. God only knows what was in it. It lay there a few seconds sizzling like a skyrocket ready to take off, then flashed and swooshed like gunpowder. Dr. Indigo rocked back on his heels and watched the mushroom shaped cloud roll up into the treetops. The fire caught his face again and I seen the light in his blue glasses and that gatory smile for the last time.

Then something come over him. Maybe he seen what he done, seen it all. A quarter million Japs good as dead and the world held hostage and all that poison set loose upon the land and maybe Jesus weeping, too.

And his smile sort of drooped and he dropped his cane and clutched his throat and took two steps forward, then two steps back and he hung there for a half a minute, dancing now with death. Then his knees buckled and he fell face first into the river beach sand.

We quit our wrastling and lay there, ear to ear, me and Harley Davidson, wondering what in the hell we just seen.

Dr. Indigo's right leg twitched a little, and when it stopped, I stood up and wobbled out into the firelight.

Harley Davidson hung there in the weeds. "Oh, Lordy, Mr. Lil Mac. I dasn't touch him!"

I wouldn't touch him either. But I bent over and looked real close. He was dead, all right. His blue glasses had flung off and his eyes were still open and they caught the light from the driftwood fire, and flickered green from sea mineral.

Chapter Twenty-One

We might have missed the first Manigault burying, but you can bet we made the second. Daddy said a Buckra root doctor sheriff might dampen proceedings at the First African Baptist, so we skipped the funeral and drove out to join the mourners at the grave. As it turned out, we didn't dampen much at all.

There was me and Daddy in the pickup, with Miss Marzette squoze between, across the Tullifinny bridge, down past where me and Harley had seen the doctor's last rooting, to the old slave cemetery along the banks of the Little Glory.

It was a beautiful and drearisome spot, where the light come down like through cathedral glass, down through a great green grove of mossy oaks along the riverbank, down through the tall yellow highground pines, through the hickories and tupelo and cedar, falling in a moving patchwork across a jungle of saw palmetto and cassena and wax myrtle.

This was a place of restless spirits, where upwards of ten generations of Negroes were laid to uneasy rest, where the ground would cry out if it could, where you would not want to go on a full moon midnight, and if you did, where you might bring home more than ticks and chiggers.

The Negroes knew better than to come here needlessly. In broad daylight, they'd hack their way into the woods with bush axes and machetes and cross-cut saws and sweat while they put a person in the ground. But after every burying, they'd clear out and let the brush take over. You could drive right by and not know there was a graveyard there at all.

We rattled to a stop and got out and followed the trail through the bushes, past graves with careening homemade stones, names and dates scratched into concrete with a nail, past graves with gub-ment stones from each of the wars the Negroes fought for us, privates and corporals and sergeants in quartermaster and engineering and transportation battalions, gassed and bayoneted and shot, past graves with no stones at all, just sad and oblong depressions in the leafy ground.

There was no flowers, no potted plants, no little American flags above the dead soldiers. The Negroes wanted the spirits to stay put, not to come home pestering for something they might-a needed. So they left whatever they thought the dead might want, likker bottles, medicine bottles, glasses, slippers, cigarettes, false teeth, and rusted up old alarm clocks stomped to disfunction at the time of death, broken pitchers, broken washbasins, a toaster, and a telephone with the receiver off the hook. There at the end of the trail was clearing and a grave with a storebought stone: "Safe in the Everlasting Arms." And beneath that legend, a name: Bo Manigault. And there beside the grave was a fresh hole and a mound of dirt and three Negroes lounging in the shade, two in work clothes, one in a suit.

They was passing around something, a pint of likker, I suppose, seeing how a burying is apt to make a man thirsty. The man in the suit pocketed it as soon as he seen who we was. "Mornin', Mr. Mac," he said. "You up to bidness?"

"We come to see Mr. Henry off," Daddy said.

Relief rolled off him like a wave. "Yessir, you set tight. He be here directly."

The First African Baptist was a half mile to the east. We could hear the singing on the seawind and the tamborines and the drums and the foot stomping that come together and sounded like a steam locomotive huffing up a long grade.

Miss Marzette was in her high heels and starting to break a sweat there in the shade, all heavy with grief and the breath of trees. "Mac," she said.

"OK, honey," Daddy said, "Let's find you a place to sit down."

There was a couple of oak blocks laying off to the side, where they had cut off a hurricane limb to get to Bo Manigault's grave. They was loaded up with red ants, but Daddy grabbed his hat and dusted one off and rolled it out of the sun and turned it on end for her to sit on. She sat there kind of red-faced and watery and knock-kneed, fanning herself with a scrub palmetto frond I cut with my jack knife.

Daddy left her there and walked back to the road, keeping an eye on things like a good cop will always do. And I did what I always seem to do. I slid over to the shade and set down and struck up with the Negroes.

"We works for the funeralizer," the man in the suit said.

"They dig and I catch."

"What you catch?" I asked.

"Why the womens!"

That didn't make much sense to me. "They run off?"

"Run off? How you talk, boy! We catch 'em when they fall out." He threw up his hands and made like he was 'bout to flip over onto his back.

"Faint? How you know when they get ready to fall out?"

"Why they waits til I gets there. I grab 'em an..." he paused and give a shy grin, "Boy, you open oyster?"

"Shore," I said, "Little Glory salty oyster. They the best."

"No, boy, I talkin' 'bout *oyster*, the kind that put lead in you pencil."

Well, that stumped me again, but I didn't let on.

"They take my han' and put it right on they breast. You ain' seen 'em?"

"No," I said.

"Uhh-uhh," he said, shaking his head with great pity. "You white folks ain' know how to funeralize."

And then Daddy come back. "They on the way," he said.

And here they come, a great and somber parade of Negroes, a hundred or more, young, old, women and men, in denim and Sunday best, in church shoes, in brogans, barefooted, the men carrying their caps if they had them, the women in them square-rigger Easter hats, all trudging silently behind a wagon drawn by a couple of switch-eared mules.

We stood aside and let them pass. The driver talked the mules through the turn and on down to trail towards the grave.

The wagon rocked and creaked along and over the sideboards. I seen the casket, shiny and fine as your grandma's table, bearing a twisted bouquet of wild Cherokee roses, wilted now in the August heat.

They wrestled the casket from the wagon and laid it over a couple of pine logs spanning the grave. We gathered round, the Negroes elbowing their way to the front, me and Daddy and Miss Marzette way back on the fringe. We all milled around a minute or two, then the preacher took off in a deep rich baritone.

"Brothers and sisters, in the midst of life we are in death...."

"Praise Jesus!" a woman hollered.

"No sooner is a man sprung up, he is cut down...."

"Amen!" the crowd come back.

"An we here today to say goodbye to our brother Dr..." He shifted gears before he got the word out, and you could hear the crowd suck a collective breath, "...Mr. Henry Manigault." Then he looked up and said, "Sisters, could you lead us in song?"

A little sparkplug of a gal in the first row threw back her head and bellered, "Anyway!"

That cued the crowd and they broke into "Anyway You Fix It, Lord."

> *Anyway, Anyway you fix it Lord,*
> *Anyway, Anyway, you fix it Lord,*
> *Anyway, Anyway you fix it Lord,*
> *It'll be all right with me.*

They stomped and swayed and worked through the verses,

"In my home won't you fix it Lord," and plugged in "church," "school," and "heart" while the woods rang and the river rippled and the Spanish moss moved with the seawind. An elderly sister seen us hanging there at the back of the crowd and gathered the three of us in her arms. "Move on up, white folks, you as good as we is."

We got as close as we could. They finished up the singing and the pallbearers slung ropes around the casket, lifted it, rolled away the logs and slowly lowered it into the ground. 'Bout the time the ropes was rattling up out of the hole, there come a shriek and the gal who cut loose with that song dove headfirst into the grave. "Oh Lawd, Oh Lawd, who gone help we now?"

The catcher jumped in with her and wrastled til her shoes fell off and her dress rose up over her fanny. He slung her back up out of the hole and was passing her off to the diggers when two more women come a-leaping and clawing and kicking for the casket. Down he went into the hole again, with the women atop him, and the dirt flew and the crowd took up a wailing like a body never heard.

The preacher set down his Bible, and the undertaker and the diggers and half a dozen other men helped sort them all out. They sat one of the women down on the dirt pile and patted her face and fanned her and kept ahold of her so she wouldn't jump back in. "Fool," somebody said, "why you do that?"

"Fool," she answered, "why you turn me loose?"

They brought out the shovels and we took turns covering him up. The diggers finished up, mounding the dirt, squaring the corners and patting the earth into a neat rectangle above the earthly remains of the great Dr. Indigo. Then the Negroes began laying stuff on the grave, the knot of wilted wild roses, his broad straw hat, his blue glasses. And then the preacher walked over from the wagon with that snake-head cane. He bent to lay it with the rest, but caught Daddy out the corner of his eye and straightened back up. "Here, Sheriff," he said, "I believe Mr. Henry would want you to have this."

Daddy looked at it a second and I looked at Miss Marzette and she looked at me and our eyes said yes and then she touched Daddy's shoulder and he reached out and took it.

And when we turned and walked toward the truck, that throng of Negroes parted before us like the Red Sea before Moses.

Daddy would walk with that snake-head cane for nearly forty years. It was flat Biblical. He healed the sick, comforted the weak, convicted the guilty, turned the innocent loose, most everything Dr. Indigo told him that day on the beach when he picked up that conch shell and said it was a call from Jesus.

I been limping most of my life, but I got me a cane I made from a stick of crepe myrtle, all gnarled and wore and fine and it's got a osprey on it and not no damn snake. That snake-head cane sets in the corner and I'll be damned if I'll pick it up, except to knock the dust off it once in a while and then I put it back down in a hurry. But here I go, getting ahead of myself again, right at the very end.

We dropped Miss Marzette off at Squinchy's and waited at the curb til she got in the door. We was pulling away when she come a-flapping back outside, hollering and waving Will Mahoney's last war headline: "U.S. A-Bombs Japs."

Well, I didn't know it then, but Miss Marzette was "makin' foot for stockin'" as the Negroes say. Daddy married her at the Church of the Cross before it started to show and I had me a momma again, and, in about six months, the little brother I had been waiting on so long. Percival Wade Hampton McCloud was a kicker and a squaller and liked to drove us crazy at first, all knotted up and bellering from the colic. But Miss Marzette doped him with catnip tea and honey, and after a few slugs of that, he never bothered us much at all.

Bodine never bothered us neither. About four months later, he got his name in the *Palmetto Post,* run over by a truck in Germany. I like to think Dr. Indigo had something to do with that.

Now you can tell me that Dr. Indigo never conjured up no atomic bomb. You can tell me Einstein figured it out and Roosevelt and later Truman got Fermi and Oppenheimer on it til they got it right.

But some folks know better. A root doctor set out to end the war and the war was over. Just like that.

And what do I believe? Well, I guess that really don't matter. Daddy carried that cane and when he set it down right before he died, I never picked it up. But just like Dr. Indigo said that day in court, I got the story. I set out to tell you and I told it good as I could.

And it's all Gospel Truth.

So help me, Jesus.

Acknowledgements

None of us works alone. Special thanks to Mary Beth and Tanya Van Pelt, mother and daughter, for their encouragement and direction. To my father, Capum Roger Pinckney X, who told me so many of these stories. To my mother, Chloe M. Pinckney, who blessed me with the genes of seven generations of journalists. To Arnold Gregory, who keeps the old magic alive. To Beek and Cathy Webb, who kept the rain off me when the rent was late. To Pete and Connie Wyrick, who believe in books. To my children, Chad, Susannah, Shelley, Laura, and Roger XII, who believed in me even when I had trouble believing in myself. And to Bill Fox and DuBose Heyward, who taught me much.